FIERY HEARTS

BEDTIME STORIES FOR THE PASSIONATE AND THE ADVENTUROUS

MARLAYNA FIRE

SACRED HOT PRESS

Fiery Hearts
Bedtime Stories for the Passionate and the Adventurous

Part of the series *Sacred Hot Quickies*

Published by Sacred Hot Press

Digital: 978-1-945868-07-8
Paperback: 978-1-945868-11-5

TABLE OF CONTENTS

CONNECTING!

**Keep up with Marlayna's new releases and get a free
Sacred Hot short story:**

https://www.sacredhot.com/newsletter/

INTRODUCTION

Spiritual being is not separate from sexual being.
Mind and body dance with heart and soul.
In this dance, you are always
Merging the celestial with the intimate:

Sacred Hot!

FIERY HEARTS IS ONE OF THE VOLUMES IN MY SERIES *SACRED Hot Quickies: Bedtime Stories for the Passionate and the Adventurous*

Sometimes short and quick is the perfect amount of heat!

SUGAR KISSES

I want my sugar in sweet kisses
and lollipop tongues across my skin.

I want my frosting in layers between you and me,
With cake as the bed for our passion.

I want more sweet whispered in my ears
and heavenly manna sprinkled in my mouth.

Let the pie in my face be from your fingers
which I will slowly lick sweet.

Folded in a meringue of light caress
and the sautéed magic of electric touch,
We hold our love, not in a to-go box,
but in an oven bed of caramel salted goodness.

SHIVER AND SHAKE

STANDING IN THE HALLWAY, MY FINGER NAIL DRAWS A LINE down his chest and I feel him shiver.

"You're teasing," he says.

"I am," I reply, loving every moment.

"Almost cruel," he says, "stringing me along."

"I know," I respond. "But know you will get the pay off."

"What do you mean?" he asks.

"I mean that dragging my luscious, red-painted fingernail across your chest, over your shoulders, and down your arms is really for me."

"What do you mean?" he asks again.

"Well every time you shiver, a wave washes over me, and I shiver and more."

My nail begins to trace the line of his jaw, moving toward half opened lips.

"More?" His eyebrow lifting.

I stop and look him in the eye.

"Yes, much … more …"

Grinning, slowly running my tongue across my bottom lip.

"When I linger my nail on your skin, I feel a slow burn begin at the tips of my fingers. My heart beats a bit faster. And the moisture begins."

"The moisture?"

"Yes, you know – where would you want moisture in me?"

I draw my finger across his bottom lip and then slowly pull my finger through my mouth.

He cannot speak, he is shivering.

I deliberately push the same finger into his mouth.

As I leisurely pull it out, I feel his tongue drag across slightly sucking, slowing the exit.

I learn forward and oh, so gently touch the tip of my tongue to his ear lobe.

This time a jump.

In light caress, I gently blow his lobe dry.

He growls.

I am getting what I want, no problem!

I whisper in his ear, "Every shiver creates white hot liquid in the place in me you know how to love so well!!"

"Damn, woman!" He growls and shifts.

I find myself pushed against the wall.

I smile mischievously.

"Hey, Babe! I am hot and wet and each shiver from you has me dripping honey just for you."

He closes his eyes and smiles, "Yummm…I can smell you."

He leans in and his lips find mine.

I realize it is a distraction of sorts because two fingers come for a honey hunt.

I am wet.

I am hot.

I offer a treat.

He growls again, and I shiver, drenching his hand.

There is a tug and pull, and his lips fuse into one with mine.

Magic is in his fingers tonight.

He pulls me down into the singular focus of wet, rubbing desire.

I groan and release, lost in the motion, lost in his hands.

Oh! Lordy! Such deliciousness!

I feel my honey drench his hand.

A tremble becomes a deep, deep pull.

He gathers me into his arms, kissing the tip of my nose.

"That was quite the shiver and shake!"

He grins and whispers into my ear his request, "Now, babe, my turn!"

I lose awareness because my release has pulled me into a cascade of release.

Liquid running down the inside of my thighs, he turns me around and pushes me against the wall with the length of his body against mine.

"You're mine," he growls into my ear.

His feet spread my feet.

I shiver as his fingers enter my honey well.

He lifts me up to my toes as his fingers dig deeper.

"Now my turn to tease you," he whispers into my ear.

His tongue warming, moistening my lobe.

His thighs leaning into me, I feel him pull back and unzip his pants.

I realize he is commando because his cock is quickly bouncing against my butt.

His hands find my pussy and push my legs further apart.

In one quick motion, his tip touches my entry.

His legs spring up and he has me fully impaled, my toes leaving the ground.

I lose count as he thrusts into me.

Thrusting deeper each time.

Pushing me harder.

Taking me down and into the full awareness of every shiver and shake.

His hardness pushing and pulling.

We are both wet and hot.

He growls, "Babe … ready?"

My body answers.

His responds.

Released to fly, we both come.

His cock pushing me over the top.

My honey drawing out his delight, sucking his cock to explode his own honey into mine.

Legs give out, creating puddles on the floor.

A final shiver and shake.

HOT, ICY HEAP

NINETY-EIGHT DEGREES OF HUMID AND HOT!

But thankfully, we are under a huge willow tree which blocks most of the sun.

An unusual cool breeze blows across our bodies bringing a bit of relief.

Me?

I'm not accustomed to this strong heat, especially accompanied with this mugginess.

I must admit I am complaining to my guy because I am literally hot and bothered.

Laying on my stomach, I can feel sweat dripping, collecting on that exquisitely sensitive spot on my lower back.

I turn to him and plead with as much earnestness as I can muster, "Sweetheart…please help me! I'm so hot!"

He with the amazing brown eyes smiles at me, replying, "Anything?"

I shake my head and urge, "Yes!" just to make sure he understands.

"Ok! But you need to close your eyes."

I do, taking a deep breath, happy he has an idea.

I feel his hand lift the hem of my tank top and I shiver as he blows lightly across my overheated skin.

Then a drop of cold water lands dead center in the small of my lower back.

My eyes fly open and he exclaims, "Eyes shut! No cheating!"

I do just that as another cold drop hits and again he blows lightly across my skin.

I shiver.

Again … another drop.

More feather breath.

Drop.

Blow.

Shiver.

I realize I am getting cool one place and hot in another.

I feel him shift and his hand lands in the hot spot on my back with a jolt of cold.

Not a drop, an ice cube.

He is rubbing a cube of ice across my lower back.

Slowly, making a journey from side to side.

Now more light breath, chilling me and heating me at the same time.

A hand gently pulls the back of my short, black skirt down a bit.

One hand pushing ice across my back.

Another hand places a piece of ice right at the top of the crevice between my butt cheeks.

I can feel a cool rivulet begin to course downward.

I shiver and twist a bit, trying to decide if maybe I'm not cool enough or if I want to be hotter still.

He stretches beside me, halting the ice journey.

I regret immediately the cessation.

"How are you, Baby?" he queries.

Hoping I will encourage him, I keep my eyes closed.

"Sweetheart, please … don't… stop. Please!"

Oh, damn! I'm begging!

"Well, there are several ways this can go. And though we are mostly hidden, we are not entirely alone."

I smile.

"Your choice! I'll go wherever you want to journey. Cool me down, make me hot. Please just don't stop!"

Thankfully the ice begins again, side to side.

I let myself sink into the back and forth motion, relaxing as his hand makes the journey.

Then his other hand returns with ice for the crevice.

This time his finger does not stop as it pushes the cube down and around, his finger pressing and massaging.

More ice, more stroking of the valley.

I am shaking, shivering. A groan escapes my throat.

"Baby, quiet! Should I stop?"

I shake my head and whisper, "No! No!"

His finger pulls away.

He lifts the bottom of my skirt, pulls the top of my panties down several inches or more, and deposits another cube into the crevice, letting the panties fall back against my skin.

His finger pushes the ice against my skin, down and around.

Through the light cotton material, he pushes the ice inside.

I want to scream!

The cold and the hot!

I twitch as his finger follows the ice cube inside.

A cool shock which almost immediately feels like a melted flow pushing past his finger.

My panties are now soaked with two kinds of moisture.

He is masterful with the tips of his fingers.

I shiver in anticipation.

Instead, he pulls his finger out.

He returns with ice down the valley of my crevice, his finger chasing the ice down, around, and inside in fluid motion.

The ice melts quickly creating more melting flow which chills and heats.

I feel sweat starting on the back of my neck and my body is alternating spots of hot and cold, sprinkled with tingly goodness.

Three more ice cubes make the valley journey in rapid succession.

I'm trying so hard to keep my eyes closed and my mouth still.

"Babe," he requests with a husky, breathy voice, "Babe, turn over!"

Up and over on to my back I go as I feel him shift as well.

My eyes remain closed.

I feel his hand come up my skirt, pushing a cube into the crotch of my panties.

I suck in breath as the chill heats, making me clench and struggle.

His hand pulls back and returns, slipping the ice past the material and into my over-heating core, instantly melting and running.

I am losing my ability to concentrate.

Now just his finger enters, pumping me back and forth, finding my wetness and my heat.

His finger begins to lightly massage my spongy mound, pulling and pushing, quickly increasing pressure, increasing speed, increasing intensity.

An insistent motion which begins to tighten me, coiling energy building deep within.

He pulls with his finger, once, twice and the coil bursts.

I feel a deep wave flow from core source in me.

I buck, his hand keeping me from twisting.

I give a mouthless scream.

I lift up as I come.

I feel him grab hold of my panties and tug, pulling them completely off.

Lifting my skirt, pulling my legs apart, I feel his mouth graze my shaking pussy lips with an ice cube.

A tiny, barely audible moan escapes my mouth.

He rubs the ice against my clit.

Hot … cold.

Hot … cold.

Wetness washes across as the ice liquifies.

His teeth nip and then he pulls my clit into his mouth, sucking intensely, tongue both hot and cold.

Now a new coil is building.

He is still sucking, and his cool finger tips are running up and down my legs.

Momentarily I wonder if anyone can see.

Then his tongue flicks, teasing, tasting.

I let go of all awareness but him and me.

He returns to sucking with a rhythm he knows focuses me into a nowhere place.

Patiently yet with intent, his tongue pokes and licks and now he is intently sucking me to the edge of coiled release.

A finger rubs on the rosebud of my ass, slips in and gently pulls in rhythm with the sucking.

A building motion, a wave ready to pound the surf.

From one vague awareness to another, waves crash on both shores and I feel orgasms hit both button and hole.

I buck and twist and come so hard I'm gasping for breath.

I roll up and pull on him, bringing his mouth to mine, tasting me on him.

On lips, on tongue, on chin.

Now more tongue.

WE COLLAPSE TOGETHER IN A PLEASANTLY HOT AND bothered heap.

IN THE BACKGROUND, I HEAR, "BRAVO! WELL DONE!"

BIRTHDAY WORKOUT

I SAY WHEN YOU'RE READY

"Bend over."

His voice is rough on the edges and I hear his deep breath as his hand reaches out and tries to gently push me over the kitchen counter.

In that one breath, I also hear his hope that I will push back.

Friday night, 6pm.

He is just home from work and a long week of meetings, negotiating, and haggling.

If you'd think he might be ready to relax you'd not be wrong.

But before he can relax, I know what he needs from me.

Ever go to the gym and get interrupted about two-thirds of the way through your workout?

You've been working hard, giving everything.

Your body and mind are looking forward to complete exhaustion and the satisfaction of giving until you're incapable of anymore because every muscle is spent.

You're jelly.

But when you're interrupted, you're robbed of the satisfaction, of the wonderful feeling of achieving the glory of *I've-pushed-so-far-I'm-in-failure* exhaustion.

I know my husband.

Just from his two words and the deep breath, I know he feels robbed of complete exhaustion.

For all that he has done this week, it wasn't quite enough.

He's feeling interrupted, still desiring complete release to bring him to the point of the satisfaction of utter exhaustion.

He's looking to me to provide, to satisfy his desire.

His fingers on my back are asking me to extend the bridge to completion.

I do what I instinctively know will bring his release.

I push back against his fingers, pushing him, causing him to dig in deeper.

Looking over my shoulder, with a teasing grin I begin our dance.

"Not so fast, Mr. Insistent!"

His fingers dig in further.

I push back more.

Shifting to the side away from those fingers, I stake my claim.

"I'm not some pansy stockbroker willing to roll over just cuz you say bend."

He growls and brings his hands to rest on my shoulders.

"Not so fast, baby! I want to get you ready for our evening out."

He has the most devastating look.

A cross between teasing, enjoyment, and intensity to get the job done.

Looking into his eyes, he fixes me with this look.

Now I know I really can't back down.

I know what he has in mind, but I also know he wants a chase, a push-back, a promise to finish the workout.

I release my push just enough to be able to completely turn around.

Now we are standing eye to eye.

"But, sugar," I begin. "I'm already to go. I've showered and pampered myself head to toe. I even have on one of your favorite dresses – just for you, sweetie!"

I've spent two hours doing all the things because it's my birthday.

Mani-pedi earlier along with some strategic sugaring.

I have coordinated everything to match my favorite dress – dark red dupioni silk with a fitted bodice and big, beautiful full skirt.

I smile as sweetly as I can because the gleam in his eye is making me warm.

Alpha male predator on the hunt for satisfaction turns me on quickly especially when I'm the focus of that hunt.

I kiss his nose and offer another, what I hope, is an innocent smile because, if I've gauged correctly, that will ignite his frustration.

He leans in and whispers a growl in my ear, "You're beautiful but you are not ready!"

His tongue reaches out and swirls around my ear lobe.

My knees weaken a bit, but my resolve strengthens because I know I've nailed his mood.

Now it's time to nail him.

"Sweetheart, I'm ready. It's time to go so we get to Gino's for our 7pm reservations."

He pulls back and stares at me with his deep brown challenging eyes.

"I don't care about timing. Tonight, I say when you're ready. And you're not ready – yet."

Determined, I push past him, knowingly egging him on.

"Don't be silly. I'm good to go."

He reaches out, snagging my hand and bringing it down against his thigh.

In the same motion, he pulls me tight to his side.

His voice rougher now, tension building, again in my ear, "Until I say you're ready, we are not going anywhere."

I turn, give him another kiss, and pull my hand away from his.

With a much lighter tone than I feel I reply, "Honey, what's up with you? I'll go get my coat."

I walk from the kitchen into the dining room, wondering what he will choose.

I feel warmth building at my core.

I'm excited to find out if what I think he wants is really what he has in mind. Though we've been down this road many a time, he still surprises me in very delicious ways.

"Ok! Enough!" he shouts. I hear his excitement building in those rough edges of his voice.

Following me, he quickly grabs firmly on to my arm and at the same time, with his other hand, he lifts a dining room chair away from the table.

Insistently, he pulls me so we stand my back to his front.

"Sweetheart," he drawls, more heat in my ear. "You know one of the reasons I love this dress is because I can do this."

In one fluid motion, one hand on the middle of my back, he pushes me against the table.

The other hand grabbing hold of the big skirt of my dark red dress and raising it up and over my head.

My backside now fully exposed.

"Well now, I can see why you might think you're ready to go. I love the red panties you have on."

His finger hooks under the elastic and I can feel his heat as his finger traces my butt.

He shifts his stance so that he is between my legs and his hand on my back presses down more, lifting me to the very edge of my toes.

I feel him lean over me, his finger kneading the edges of my panties.

He whispers, "I'm going to make you ready."

I wiggle under his weight like I'm trying to get away though knowing that I neither can nor want to escape.

His finger follows the edge of my panties until his finger is between my legs.

The tip of his finger slides up and down my slit.

I feel moisture beginning to collect.

I twist and push against his hand. But he has me firmly in hand.

"Ready?" he asks with no intention of waiting for my response.

I know this excites him and he knows this forcefulness excites me.

His finger slips between and into the core of my heat.

Pushing, exploring, he fingers me raising more heat.

"Ah sweetie! You're so wet already. I feel you beginning to drip."

His finger pumps in and out.

I try hard not to move away from this wonderful sensation.

But I do push back against his hand on my back and feel the hard length of him against my butt.

He whispers in my ear, "You're giving me much to think about tonight."

His heated breath adds to my excitement.

He fingers me harder and deeper, then pulls out of me.

I whimper because I'm not ready for him to stop.

Once begun, I always want more.

He chuckles.

"Yes, honey. I know you want more – but I have no intention of doing any more until you're thoroughly ready. And as I've said already, I'm the one who decides when you are ready."

He shifts his body, drawing my legs a little further apart, lifting my toes off the ground.

He pulls the edge of my panties to the side.

I feel the broad smooth surface of something up against my slit.

A little bigger than a golf ball.

"Ready to finish getting dressed? I have something for you to keep warm for me tonight."

Before I can reply, I feel a push and the hard smoothness is lodged inside of me.

Bending back over me, he licks my ear.

"Do not remove!" His whisper harsh and demanding.

His finger finds my clit.

He pushes and pulls.

The sensation is mind-blowing, and I follow, feeling myself losing any control, ready to follow wherever he will take me.

And yes, I do want him to take me.

Warmth is gathering and I feel myself begin to let go ready to explode.

But he stops, leaving me on the brink.

"Yep! Now you're ready to go."

He lifts up, his hand grazing my back.

Leaning his thighs up against my still bare ones, his hands caress my butt. Very carefully he pulls the skirt of my dress down.

Patting my butt some more, he says, "I love this dress. It hides what is only for me."

Standing and turning, I find a grin on his face.

"Feeling full already?" he asks.

Reaching forward, I press my hand on his shaft and gently palm his tip.

I reach up and catch his lip between my teeth as my hand lightly squeezes.

"Game on, Mr. Insistent!" I whisper, as I release his lip.

He pulls me to him, hands on my butt, pulling me in closer.

Sinking his mouth to mine, tongue taking me down, time evaporating.

I enjoy the dive especially as his hands begin to slowly move up the sides of my body.

I let my hand snake across his harness, taking as much as I can into my hands through his dress pants.

I tug and look him in the eye.

"Bet I can last longer than you!" I challenge.

"You're on!" he whispers.

The smoothness within me begins a very slow vibration almost unnoticeable except for his next words.

"Babe, this night is just for you." He smiles mischievously.

"I am going to make you cum during dinner. Maybe during the salad. Maybe during dessert. Maybe both. But there, in the middle of the restaurant, in front of everyone, you will lose it – and only I will know because I will have you without even touching you."

His smile is deep and his eyes full of heat as the vibrating motion slowly speeds up.

I can't not notice how the vibration is lighting a fire within me.

My knees shake.

I have to put my hand on the table to keep from falling.

He has now described the challenge and how he intends to finish his workout.

"Well," I begin. "I don't think you'll last and that will be much more embarrassing for you than for me."

I give his cock another pull.

I accept his challenge.

"With just a bit more attention, I can get you off before we even walk out the door."

He laughs and steps back.

"Nope, not time for me. But it is time to go."

He smooths my hair, runs his finger along my lips.

"You are beautiful. And now you are ready!"

The vibration within me comes to a full stop as he ushers me out the door and into the car.

DESSERT'S ON ME

As we pull into the restaurant parking lot, he turns to me.

"Baby, I love you! Hope you enjoy tonight."

I kiss him and pull back, "No worries! Tonight, is going to be great!"

He gets out of the car and comes around to open my door, offering his hand.

I've been looking forward to celebrating with our two closest friends.

"I mean it," he whispers. "Enjoy tonight!"

His hand squeezes mine and the vibration begins at a slow staccato beat.

As I walk, I feel the shaking sides rubbing my insides with a gentle yet insistent shake.

I start to fall into the motion within and catch my toe.

He steadies me, his hand to my elbow.

"Steady sweetie! No need to get shook up."

The vibration stops again.

But I am still shaking, my core at a low boil, in anticipation of when he might begin again.

At the restaurant entrance, he offers our name to the maître d' who unexpectedly leads us to a private dining room at the back of the restaurant.

He goes through the door first and again offers his hand.

As I enter, the whole room erupts in shouts and laughter.

"Surprise! Happy Birthday!"

Maybe twenty people sitting at a long table with two empty places halfway along the length on opposite sides.

Everyone stands up and turns towards me, yelling best wishes.

Hands clapping.

Little paper birthday horns noisily rolling in and out as the crowd begins towards me.

I turn to look at my husband and he pulls me into a big hug and whispers in my ear, "Happy Birthday, Sweetheart!"

He kisses me and whispers, "Have a great time! But know I will be thinking of you!"

I feel a quick, inner, intense shake and the grin I see on his face is pure delight.

I feel other hands on my shoulder and turn to embrace my friends.

We laugh and hug.

Everyone full of joy and excited to celebrate my birthday.

My husband begins ushering us to the table as waiters appear with trays of filled champagne flutes.

"A toast for the Birthday Girl!" he yells.

Everyone cheers and raises their glasses in anticipation of his words.

"You, sweetheart, are the love of my life. You bring magic to all you know and make the world an awesome place through all you do. May your heart always find peace and love. May each day of your life be happy and exciting. Please find it in your heart to walk with me always. Happy Birthday, honey! I love you!"

I blow him a kiss, "Thank you, sweet man! You are my love always!"

I see his hand go into his coat pocket and he mouths, "Thank you!"

I feel a heavy jolt and then another push at my inner walls.

I feel myself heat up and a blush begins across my cheeks.

I feel myself begin to tip and am trying desperately to hold back the tide.

"Ahh!" my best friend yells out. "Look she's blushing!"

Everyone claps and cheers.

"There's nothing to be embarrassed about," someone calls out. "We are so happy for you both!"

My husband clears his throat, hiding that mischievous grin, "Alright, everyone! Let's sit down for dinner."

Dinner begins and so does the conversation.

Everyone is having a great time.

About halfway through my salad, I look at my husband sitting across the table from me, remembering his promise.

He is engaged with the person next to him.

I thought he would have started something by now, but he has been quiet.

I realize I'm tight with anticipation.

Dinner is delicious and every course, my friends are changing seats so that I get a chance to speak with everyone.

I feel my phone vibrate and take a quick look to see a message from my husband.

> *I am hard just thinking of you.*
>
> *I know you're ready, but are you ready?*

I text back:

> *Bring it on, Mr. Insistent!*
>
> *You're going down ... or should I say off?*

I look up and he winks at me.

The vibration begins a smooth buzz.

I turn to talk with the person who just sat down by me.

I try my best to ignore the buzz.

But it's not stopping, and I am feeling distracted.

"What are your plans for this year?"

I realize my friend is directing the question to me.

The vibration intensifies into a syncopated rhythm of short-long-long, short-long-long.

The beat drags me in.

No matter how I try to squeeze or relax, the size of the smoothness makes it impossible to avoid the effect.

I can feel waves beginning to build.

I can feel this wonderful bubbling at my core.

My cheeks are warming.

I can feel my nipples standing up, wanting to get into the game.

The vibration is a wonderful inner workout.

My friend looks at me with question on her face. Then she smiles quickly and touches my arm.

"Oh! Don't worry! That's too much of a question right now. Let's get together next week and talk!"

I smile my agreement as the vibration begins to overwhelm me.

I feel a very deep heat beginning to build.

The vibration shifts to a steady pulse which zips me up even further.

I look across the table at my husband.

He is laughing with a friend.

I watch him slip his hand into his pocket.

I tense, waiting.

The pulse intensifies as does the grin on his face.

He knows what he is doing.

Now I am the person mid-workout.

I feel the heat build.

I feel my body preparing to spring.

I don't know what I'll do when I am pushed beyond.

But I've decided not to worry.

I can feel myself getting ready to explode.

Then the pulse stops.

Nothing.

I feel jerked back from a cliff.

Cheeks flushed, trying not to pant.

My husband stands up, clinging his knife against his wine glass.

"Okay everyone! Time for dessert! Let's get some more champagne for the Birthday Girl, first!"

Someone fills my glass. The lights in the room go out.

"Honey, close your eyes!" I do as everyone makes a collective "Ooooh!"

I feel a hand on my shoulder and my husband whispers in my ear, "Open your eyes."

I do.

The waiter sets a flaming chocolate cake down in front of me.

My favorite cake of all time: brandy-infused chocolate cream frosting with the ooey-gooey goodness of salted caramel, piled high on a flourless fudge cake.

My husband sets down a lit tall red candle with a Happy Birthday sign hanging in front.

He really knows what I like: that the flambé shouldn't exclude the requisite birthday candle.

All my friends join together and sing the Happy Birthday song for me.

I watch the flame on the cake dance and slowly die down.

I look at everyone, kiss my husband, and look back at the cake.

I feel the vibration begin at a very slow, light pulse.

I want to settle in and enjoy the ride.

Instead, I pause and make a wish, and with a big breath blow out the large red candle.

Still failing to ignore my inner buzz.

As the cake is sliced and served, the vibration goes again to a syncopated pulse.

I savor the warm caramel in the cake as I savor the heated pulse at my core.

I feel the wet heat begin to build as I lick the chocolate from my fork.

The pulse begins a new, full-pound intensity and my fork full of cake falters on the way to my mouth.

Finally, in the bite goes and I slowly lick the fork clean as a way to cover the urge to moan.

I am so wet I don't need licking anywhere else.

Now the pulse begins a steady, insistent, rhythmic beat.

I'm trying my best to make it look like I'm completely engulfed by the cake.

Each bite gives me a moment to focus on the cliff building within.

Each lick of frosting, a moment to savor the deliciousness of heat oozing, bubbling up.

The heated caramel across my tongue hits at just the moment the vibration kicks up another notch.

"So yummy," I declare, heat on my cheeks.

Another bite of cake and the vibration now is an urgent, intense pulse unlike anything I've ever felt before.

I feel like the smoothness is my husband, pounding me from within, hitting the depths of all that can possibly trigger euphoric release.

I look at my plate and stifle a gasp.

Only one more bite.

I dare not look up.

I stare at the bite.

I feel myself being pulled forward by every subtle, intense motion within.

Whatever is pounding my core has fused with me.

My core now lit and heated like the caramel and the cake.

Flame dancing and wanting to explode.

I feel the tip at the top. Energy gathering.

I start to lift fork to mouth but before I can the pulse turns to a slam and pushes me over the cliff.

"OOoooohhh!" I scream, feeling the explosion within as wet, warm, delicious gush of juicy icing.

I shove the last bite in my mouth as my core continues to heat.

Lightning flashes, core ripped open by a huge pulse of motion.

I cum so hard I have to stop all else, riding waves.

More vibration insists.

I cum again sending a river across my entire body.

Overheated, yet gasping as quietly as possible to not draw attention.

I slowly, pull the fork from my mouth, finished, spent, still tingling.

"Damn!" I exclaim. "That was the best dessert ever!"

I look at my husband. "You're next!"

My friends all cheer thinking I'm referring to his birthday.

A BUTTERFLY SPREAD

As we leave the dining room, I excuse myself and head for the ladies' room.

When I return, I find my husband and quickly deposit the panty-wrapped vibrator into his hand.

He startles a bit as he realizes what is now with him and quickly fumbles it into his pocket.

"I was serious." I whisper in his ear. "Your turn next!"

Everyone now thanked and hugged, we head for our car.

"Are you ready?" I teasingly inquire.

"Not quite. Gotta get us home, first."

"Ok," I respond. "Then just watch."

I sit in the front passenger seat, drop my shoes on the car floor, and lift my feet on to the dash.

As my husband sits down and begins to turn on the car, I ask, "Remember why you like this dress?"

I look him in the face as I slowly pull back the wide skirt of my dress, revealing my smoothness from toes on up.

"Better watch where you're driving." I suggest as I slowly spread my knees.

I hear a growl.

I watch him as I lick my finger and then reach down, slowly inserting my finger.

More growling.

I can smell myself.

I think he can, too.

The entire evening returning, as I realize it takes little to re-ignite my wet warmth.

I pull out my finger and looking at him, I lightly lick my finger before inserting it fully into my mouth.

"Damn! You're killing me!" He growls.

I smile trying to match his mischievous grins of before with one of my own.

I pull my finger from my mouth and reach down again into my now re-heated core.

I watch his face as I pump my finger in and out.

I pull out and, shifting in my seat, I lean over and gently insert my finger in his mouth.

"I know you are full – but here's a little treat just for you!" I tease.

A brake, a growl, a tongue on my finger.

He gently bites down and his teeth pull across my finger as I gently withdraw, amazed he is still keeping us safe on the road.

I'm thinking he is wishing we had gotten a lift so he could concentrate on me.

"Baby, you taste so good!" he whispers.

I turn forward in my seat, pulling my skirt down.

"No more?" he asks.

"No. Not now. You're going to have to wait."

COMPLETE

As we pull into our driveway, I make a request.

Just the thought of my ask lights my fire once more.

"I'd like for your dessert to begin and end in two different places. And both places are your choice."

"OK!" he agrees.

I watch him begin to consider.

The car stops in the garage.

I open the door and jump out.

"But you gotta catch me first!"

I dash in the door to the house, moving as fast as I can.

I sprint down the hallway, past the kitchen, and through the family room where I kick off my shoes.

I hear the car door slam.

Then nothing.

No footsteps.

I tip toe into the dining room and look through the door into the kitchen and see nothing.

Still on my tip toes, I creep by the end of the kitchen counter focused on the living room.

"Hello."

I jump and turn towards the voice. My husband, barefoot, jacket hanging in his hand.

That grin is on his face and he is coming at me.

Jacket left behind.

"I have chosen the first place," he says. Voice rough on the edges, raised breath though I know he hasn't been running.

"Oh! You have?" I question. "Where's that?" My voice going a little high at the end.

"Here."

He takes hold of my shoulders and marches me backward until my butt bumps into the breakfast table.

He leans down and captures my mouth with his.

His tongue sliding in and tickling, raising my heat.

Pressed front to front, I can feel his hard shaft pushing against me.

Without a word, he turns me around.

"Bend over."

Now, full circle, we return to where we began.

His hand insistent against my back, giving me no choice but to follow his command.

I feel his legs lean against me.

Next one leg then another as he steps out of his pants, his hand keeping me pinned on the table.

I squirm a bit and press into him, but his hand keeps me in one place.

"I. Want. More."

He demands with determination.

He lifts the skirt of my dress and quickly pushes his finger into my pussy.

Several insistent pumps and he pulls out.

I hear his lips smacking.

"Yum! You're so sweet!"

He pushes me further on to the table and lifts my feet up, stepping between my spread legs and then pulls me toward him.

From one second to the next, I go from wet and empty to wet and full.

He shoves his cock into me and pulls himself almost out and waits.

The anticipation begins to unhinge me from time and space.

My only focus is him and how he wants to take us beyond.

My breath in is interrupted by his motion away and then quickly in.

Heated smoothness filling me, pushing me, drilling me to the table.

He fills me completely.

The pulse of him and me beginning to rise.

He usually likes to take his time but tonight there is a raw determination flowing from him which is lifting me up and building another mountain, another peak.

I let go and feel myself zero in on him and his motion, in and out.

He is building a path for us both, picking up the pace and the force.

An exquisite journey.

Fast in, slow out.

Slow in, fast out.

Each random shove, hitting the very depth of me.

His hands now on my hips.

Pace more a sprint than a climb.

Like the last few yards of a race.

A delicious pound in.

Now another, in and out.

I feel myself begin to fly.

As I hear him cry out, his last shove in tips my balance.

We are now both yelling in the ecstasy of climbing and then falling together.

Another shove and I explode again.

He falls on top of me, breathing hard.

I'm jelly.

I can feel his pounding heart.

The weight of him holds me close.

"I'm not done with you, baby," he whispers.

He gathers me up and takes me to our bedroom.

Stripping off my dress and bra, he pushes me onto the bed.

I feel light as a feather.

"Before I finish, I want to lick the frosting," he whispers.

"Ah, sugar!"

He buries his mouth on my still wet slit.

His tongue pushes in as his finger pulls on my clit.

"Honey," I start.

But his insistent tongue steals my words.

He is always able to push me beyond – further than I think I can go.

Now his tongue shifts to an insistent pull on my clit.

Teeth nipping, pushing.

Fingers now entering and pulling up.

Tongue returning to dig in.

Back and forth, finger dig, clit bit.

Suck.

Pull.

Lick.

Again.

More.

Push.

I feel another melting building.

Caramel burning, icing scorched.

This man is working me over.

This man is pushing me past my limits.

This man celebrating me ... us.

I hear him growl.

"Baby ... damn!"

He stands up.

His cock at just the right level for delivery.

He pushes my knees into my chest.

His cock brushes my entry.

I take in those gorgeous eyes and that awesome grin.

His eyes fix on mine.

He shoves in filling me to the very bottom.

Such a delicious push.

I stare back, inviting him in, daring him to bring more.

His effort focused entirely on me.

His gaze lights my fire.

I am flame!

I am glowing just for him.

His cock sinks in again and our fire is now properly stoked ... again.

His shaft hits my deepest inner wall and like an instant spark, I ignite.

I feel him momentarily still and then he yells, "Sugar, mine!"

He shoves again and explodes fully, completely pushed to the hilt.

A deep wave quivers across my body and I squeeze down on him feeling him let go.

Reciprocating.

Reverberating.

Both of us now absolutely spent.

Heavy breath, hearts beating.

Somehow, he pulls me into his arms and lifts us both up and further on to the bed.

He kisses my cheek.

We settle into a wonderful cuddle bundle.

"Thanks for my dessert," he whispers.

He pulls me close.

"Happy Birthday, sugar! I love you," he whispers.

I smile and close my eyes as I push my butt into him.

Nestled, satisfied, ready to dream.

We are an exhausted, happy, wet heap.

Workout finally complete.

RIVER BED

WORK WAS EXHAUSTING TODAY.

I do what I love – my work is one of my primary passions.

But sometimes, some days, the thrill, the push to connect, the ability to find the next horizon saps my energy.

Like a good workout or a long hike, I spend all in happy, excited, exhilarating connection.

Now I find myself doing what I fantasized about doing as I drove home.

My shoes are left at the front door, my purse dumped there as well. Jacket on the floor.

Large glass of sake on my nightstand.

Work clothes shed and pooled on the floor.

Me, lying on my bed in my white cotton robe. Book beside me, falling just beyond my fingertips.

As I take a deep breath, I let go and take stock.

How do I feel?

What do I need?

Another deep breath and I feel my body untighten and relax.

Bent knees flop open and the cool air touches my lips.

I feel my belly and slide my hand lower, over the bushy curls.

I smile at myself and the back-and-forth desires I have about liking to be both waxed bare and sporting dark curls.

I have worked diligently with myself to be open in my sexual expression.

I didn't get much support on this as a young woman.

I've had to explore this jungle on my own.

But now I feel much more confident and openly eager to explore the sexual depths of me.

I lightly stroke my curls feeling the smooth strands slightly moist from the exertion of the day.

A growing need for release.

I'm not in a hurry.

I sip my sake.

I comb the curling strands and spread my knees further.

I stick the tip of my finger into my sake and suck the liquid into my mouth.

The coolness of the liquor balanced with a slight heat as it rushes down my throat is delicious.

I run my tongue across my lips to distribute the taste.

My finger dips again into the sake and I reach lower this time in between my curls and lightly anoint my clit with the warming liqueur.

My clit wiggles a bit in the coolness and warms to attention.

I gently caress and settle into my pillows as I feel heat radiate.

My nipples beg for attention.

I tug at both with sake-laced fingertips.

More heat gathers.

Then I feel a warm breath at my ear and the voice of my lover whispers. "Can I help you, baby?"

I stretch from toes to crown like a cat and nod my approval.

Though I had been so focused I hadn't realized he had gotten home, I know why he has volunteered to help.

He gets so much peace and joy being both witness and participant in my relaxing release.

He can be here for me, and for me only.

No tit for tat demand will be issued.

He has helped me learn that a me-only experience is not selfish, but self-loving.

I feel his finger gently brush my clit.

Lightly, wet with liquid which feels like the sake.

I stretch again content because I know he knows.

He won't rush me; he has learned my time.

His finger lightly caresses my clit with tender motion.

I can feel my heat begin to pick up like a river swelling with light steady raindrops.

A steady beat, without anticipation yet full of intent.

Light, firm, short, long, a push, a drive, a pulling back, now a push back.

His fingers dance across the bed of my heating places, pulling at each nipple first with fingers, and then with teeth.

A dance to begin that which proceeds without worry of end.

I sink into his motion with me, no expectations, no concern.

Now, his finger, his tongue, my core.

He begins to build the rhythm just as he knows I adore.

I don't like to be pushed to perform.

I like to be played like a never-ending tune of joy.

I feel the thrill of the tune build with short little shivers of pleasure which prophesize the crescendo.

I push my core into his fingers and his lapping tongue.

A short gasp.

A longer swell.

The exertion of my day focused but as a river of comfort in this moment.

Here, now, just his finger and my heat.

I think he can feel the brink building within me, because he whispers, "Come for me, baby. Come for me!"

Like a warm riverbed heated in the sun, light gathers, and I explode leaving behind any awareness of the bed or the river.

I come for me.

QUARTETTO

The whole of this story appeared when I got to a certain point in my writing and thought of multiple endings. Not wanting to choose, I have put each end within a repeated tease for the reader.

PRIMO

NOT QUITE AWAKE, I FEEL THE MORNING SUN ACROSS MY BED, but I don't feel the firm body which is usually my first morning sensation.

Instead, I feel a warm wet tongue across my lips and as I shift for a better angle, I startle awake.

I can't move!

My hands are firmly above and my ankles firmly below.

I hear a chuckle and I turn toward the sound and realize I can't see.

The moment hits me: He has butterflied me.

My ankles and wrists bound.

My eyes covered.

Now his tongue questions and I respond, opening, allowing him in.

I love his surprises and realize I'm already excited to see where he leads.

A finger begins a light trail up one arm, tickling, stimulating warmth everywhere.

Then the finger lights on a knee and moves towards my toe.

Again, heat flushes and I involuntarily squirm.

I have no idea where this is headed.

His lips return to mine and the tenderness is breathtaking.

The growl of his desire lifts my center off the bed and I groan in return.

The bed shifts and now his tongue is licking my other lips.

I feel liquid heat begin to flow.

His tongue becomes insistent and pushy and firm.

I buck trying to push forward and retreat all in one flow.

He responds with a finger in and a pull up and push down and I buck again.

Suddenly the finger is gone.

I am left hanging halfway off a cliff of heated desire.

No movement, heat removed.

But…yet a sound.

Something warm and hard is pushed into the slit of my lower lips.

A muffled sound joins a steady vibration, re-igniting, inflaming, my core liquid running.

The bed shifts, and I gasp as tongue touches nipple.

Teeth gently grasp and tug upward and down.

That tongue lightly licks, teasing.

The sensation is exquisite and warm.

My core shivers in response.

Then…all stops.

No vibration.

No tongue.

No teasing.

I test my bindings and find them still there, keeping me spread on the bed.

I whimper.

I pull.

I find no relief.

Turning, pulling I try to get some sense of anything.

Five minutes, maybe more, passes.

Nothing.

I am awake but floating.

Aware of being displayed.

Aware of being brought to the brink, then stymied.

Now, what?

Then a faint feeling at my center begins to stimulate what I realize remains.

The feeling intensifies.

The hardness I feel is coming to attention and shaking, hitting all the receivers located in my now re-warming core.

The vibration is waking all that was ignited and then disappointed.

I shiver.

I shake.

My core re-heats and the vibration intensifies and begins a staccato beat.

My liquid begins to flow again.

My nipples stiffen.

I buck as the vibration pulses hard and insistent.

I lift my hips trying to lean into whatever might send me riding an edge between warmth of here and the forever bliss of exploding heat pushed beyond.

But before I exit, the vibration stops, and the cliff abruptly disappears — again.

I am left hanging, bucking, trying to catch the ride which has vanished once more.

My skin is heated, lined with moisture which in the sudden absence leaves me cold as moisture evaporates.

I growl in frustration and pull at my bindings.

Still splayed.

Still stymied.

Still frustrated.

I scream, "Make me come, you bastard, make me come!"

Nothing.

No sound.

No motion.

Nothing.

I growl in angering frustration.

Unable to move.

Unable to find relief.

I squirm, hoping any motion might be enough to tip the balance, knowing, realizing it is not enough.

Exhausted, I fall asleep, unfinished.

SECONDO

Not quite awake, I feel the morning sun across my bed, but I don't feel the firm body which is usually my first morning sensation.

Instead, I feel a warm wet tongue across my lips and as I shift for a better angle, I startle awake.

I can't move!

My hands are firmly above and my ankles firmly below.

I hear a chuckle and I turn toward the sound and realize I can't see.

The moment hits me: He has butterflied me.

My ankles and wrists bound.

My eyes covered.

Now his tongue questions and I respond, opening, allowing him in.

I love his surprises and realize I'm already excited to see where he leads.

A finger begins a light trail up one arm, tickling, stimulating warmth everywhere.

Then the finger lights on a knee and moves towards my toe.

Again, heat flushes and I involuntarily squirm.

I have no idea where this is headed.

His lips return to mine and the tenderness is breathtaking.

The growl of his desire lifts my center off the bed and I groan in return.

The bed shifts and now his tongue is licking my other lips.

I feel liquid heat begin to flow.

His tongue becomes insistent and pushy and firm.

I buck trying to push forward and retreat all in one flow.

He responds with a finger in and a pull up and push down and I buck again.

Suddenly the finger is gone.

I am left hanging halfway off a cliff of heated desire.

No movement, heat removed.

But…yet a sound.

Something warm and hard is pushed into the slit of my lower lips.

A muffled sound joins a steady vibration, re-igniting, inflaming, my core liquid running.

The bed shifts, and I gasp as tongue touches nipple.

Teeth gently grasp and tug upward and down.

That tongue lightly licks, teasing.

The sensation is exquisite and warm.

My core shivers in response.

Then…all stops.

No vibration.

No tongue.

No teasing.

I test my bindings and find them still there, keeping me spread on the bed.

I whimper.

I pull.

I find no relief.

Turning, pulling I try to get some sense of anything.

Five minutes, maybe more, passes.

Nothing.

I am awake but floating.

Aware of being displayed.

Aware of being brought to the brink, then stymied.

Now, what?

Then a faint feeling at my center begins to stimulate what I realize remains.

The feeling intensifies.

The hardness I feel is coming to attention and shaking, hitting all the receivers located in my now re-warming core.

The vibration is waking all that was ignited and then disappointed.

I shiver.

I shake.

My core re-heats and the vibration intensifies and begins a staccato beat.

My liquid begins to flow again.

My nipples stiffen.

I buck as the vibration pulses hard and insistent.

I lift my hips trying to lean into whatever might send me riding an edge between warmth of here and the forever bliss of exploding heat pushed beyond.

But before I exit, the vibration stops, and the cliff abruptly disappears.

I am left hanging, bucking, trying to catch the ride which has vanished once more.

My skin is heated, lined with moisture which in the sudden absence leaves me cold as moisture evaporates.

I growl in frustration and pull at my bindings.

Still splayed.

Still stymied.

Still frustrated.

I scream, "Make me come, you bastard, make me come!"

I hear a chuckle.

The vibration resumes full tilt.

A tongue re-visits my nipple and a finger lightly rubs the other.

Fingers push into my pussy and pull, heating me, making me shake.

Now teeth nip the first nipple and pull.

I buck.

I pull.

I lose any other awareness except his teeth and his hands and the increasing pulsing within.

Now a finger brushes my clit, the button of my desire.

Warm wetness pushes and pulls and suddenly teeth have captured my button, pulling, lifting me into the air.

More pull, both button and tits.

More tongue joining the pulsing and ….

Boom!

Explosion everywhere.

Button, boobs, and bursting core.

More pull, more tongue, more twisting fingers.

The second blast and the tongue doesn't stop and neither do the fingers.

Before I can scream, the fingers and tongue work like a charm.

My whole being explodes again and again and again.

I lose track of everything as the heat receives me screaming, bucking, leaving any awareness of bindings behind.

TERZO

Not quite awake, I feel the morning sun across my bed, but I don't feel the firm body which is usually my first morning sensation.

Instead, I feel a warm wet tongue across my lips and as I shift for a better angle, I startle awake.

I can't move!

My hands are firmly above and my ankles firmly below.

I hear a chuckle and I turn toward the sound and realize I can't see.

The moment hits me: He has butterflied me.

My ankles and wrists bound.

My eyes covered.

Now his tongue questions and I respond, opening, allowing him in.

I love his surprises and realize I'm already excited to see where he leads.

A finger begins a light trail up one arm, tickling, stimulating warmth everywhere.

Then the finger lights on a knee and moves towards my toe.

Again, heat flushes and I involuntarily squirm.

I have no idea where this is headed.

His lips return to mine and the tenderness is breathtaking.

The growl of his desire lifts my center off the bed and I groan in return.

The bed shifts and now his tongue is licking my other lips.

I feel liquid heat begin to flow.

His tongue becomes insistent and pushy and firm.

I buck trying to push forward and retreat all in one flow.

He responds with a finger in and a pull up and push down and I buck again.

Suddenly the finger is gone.

I am left hanging halfway off a cliff of heated desire.

No movement, heat removed.

But...yet a sound.

Something warm and hard is pushed into the slit of my lower lips.

A muffled sound joins a steady vibration, re-igniting, inflaming, my core liquid running.

The bed shifts, and I gasp as tongue touches nipple.

Teeth gently grasp and tug upward and down.

That tongue lightly licks, teasing.

The sensation is exquisite and warm.

My core shivers in response.

Then...all stops.

No vibration.

No tongue.

No teasing.

I test my bindings and find them still there, keeping me spread on the bed.

I whimper.

I pull.

I find no relief.

Turning, pulling I try to get some sense of anything.

Five minutes, maybe more, passes.

Nothing.

I am awake but floating.

Aware of being displayed.

Aware of being brought to the brink, then stymied.

Now, what?

Then a faint feeling at my center begins to stimulate what I realize remains.

The feeling intensifies.

The hardness I feel is coming to attention and shaking, hitting all the receivers located in my now re-warming core.

The vibration is waking all that was ignited and then disappointed.

I shiver.

I shake.

My core re-heats and the vibration intensifies and begins a staccato beat.

My liquid begins to flow again.

My nipples stiffen.

I buck as the vibration pulses hard and insistent.

I lift my hips trying to lean into whatever might send me riding an edge between warmth of here and the forever bliss of exploding heat pushed beyond.

But before I exit, the vibration stops, and the cliff abruptly disappears.

I am left hanging, bucking, trying to catch the ride which has vanished once more.

My skin is heated, lined with moisture which in the sudden absence leaves me cold as moisture evaporates.

I growl in frustration and pull at my bindings.

Still splayed.

Still stymied.

Still frustrated.

I scream, "Make me come, you bastard, make me come!"

I hear a chuckle.

I hear a laugh.

I feel a finger slowly tracing a line from hip bone up to the very tip of my nipple.

The finger brushes the tip, first lightly, and then with more insistence.

Then a second finger does the same, hip to tip, first lightly then more intently.

Now both fingers rubbing the very tips, alternating between light touch and a twist and pull.

At the same time, a finger on each inner thigh and I twist slightly, both hesitant and eager for where these fingers might go.

Quickly both are inserted into my nether lips. Each pulls me open.

I feel a light breeze blow across my opening.

In a quick motion, the pulsing something is quickly removed.

The fingers both top and bottom step back leaving me in the pulsing of my own body ready to come.

The bed moves as knees fill the space between my still splayed and bound legs.

This time what enters me is not plastic or pulsing.

Instead it is hard and big, the mushroom end opens me further and my nipples remember, hardening further almost to pain.

I feel this luscious cock push to the bottom of me, rubbing every cell and membrane, introducing itself to my cervix.

Such a luscious feeling!

Slowly drawing back, the mushroom pops out.

I feel a regret at the departure and hope for return.

Knees shuffle around me, I can't make out what exactly is moving and how.

Yet quickly I feel a re-entry – yet different somehow than before.

Hard, firm, but the mushroom ridge is fuller, thicker and it pushes in not as deeply, but my lips are pushed further apart.

Different yet still hugely satisfying.

In and out.

In and out.

I gasp as fingers grasp my nipples, twisting and pulling.

Teeth take hold of one.

I growl and try to buck but the weight of the shaft holds me down.

Shaft again retrieved.

Me still unsatisfied.

More knees moving and now I return to the feeling before of the other mushroom pushing all the way to the bottom, banging, bouncing, clearly desiring to find the deep pull for us both.

My hips are lifted, and a pillow settled underneath as the shaft pushes even more deeply.

The speed picks up and the length hardens within my liquid heat.

Pushing me in, pulling me out.

The heat lights me, disconnecting me from control, connecting me only to the pounding here, now.

Together we explode.

Me reaching into a darkness suddenly filled with white light.

Now tongue on my pussy lips, licking, sucking, draining me of shared delight.

Knees moving, bed bouncing, and I track back a bit to realize the fatter mushroom is back in, taking its turn.

Fingers pull at my nipples and teeth graze, nipping.

Beyond conscious choice, my body reacts and re-ignites.

I take in the thick fullness of this second shaft which does not enter fully.

Instead shallow pushes, teasing.

Then it pulls fully out and rests, cushioning my lips.

Fingers lightly stroke my inner thighs and I take a deep breath.

In my next inhale, a hard shaft pushes all the way to my hilt, pulls almost out and rams in once again.

Nerve endings I thought spent, tingle in hard waving motions across my entire body.

I feel myself both focusing and letting go.

Focus on the shaft, letting go of however I might think I can control my reaction, my response.

One, two, three more confident slams and I feel the mushroom explode, taking me along, pushing me into free fall.

The depth of my response shakes me to the core

The release relieves me of awareness.

I sink into a cloud of utter and complete bliss, bound no more.

Two bodies cradling me.

Two lips kissing me.

As one, we fall asleep.

QUARTO

Not quite awake, I feel the morning sun across my bed, but I don't

feel the firm body which is usually my first morning sensation.

Instead, I feel a warm wet tongue across my lips and as I shift for a better angle, I startle awake.

I can't move!

My hands are firmly above and my ankles firmly below.

I hear a chuckle and I turn toward the sound and realize I can't see.

The moment hits me: He has butterflied me.

My ankles and wrists bound.

My eyes covered.

Now his tongue questions and I respond, opening, allowing him in.

I love his surprises and realize I'm already excited to see where he leads.

A finger begins a light trail up one arm, tickling, stimulating warmth everywhere.

Then the finger lights on a knee and moves towards my toe.

Again, heat flushes and I involuntarily squirm.

I have no idea where this is headed.

His lips return to mine and the tenderness is breathtaking.

The growl of his desire lifts my center off the bed and I groan in return.

The bed shifts and now his tongue is licking my other lips.

I feel liquid heat begin to flow.

His tongue becomes insistent and pushy and firm.

I buck trying to push forward and retreat all in one flow.

He responds with a finger in and a pull up and push down and I buck again.

Suddenly the finger is gone.

I am left hanging halfway off a cliff of heated desire.

No movement, heat removed.

But … yet a sound.

Something warm and hard is pushed into the slit of my lower lips.

A muffled sound joins a steady vibration, re-igniting, inflaming, my core liquid running.

The bed shifts, and I gasp as tongue touches nipple.

Teeth gently grasp and tug upward and down.

That tongue lightly licks, teasing.

The sensation is exquisite and warm.

My core shivers in response.

Then...all stops.

No vibration.

No tongue.

No teasing.

I test my bindings and find them still there, keeping me spread on the bed.

I whimper.

I pull.

I find no relief.

Turning, pulling I try to get some sense of anything.

Five minutes, maybe more, passes.

Nothing.

I am awake but floating.

Aware of being displayed.

Aware of being brought to the brink, then stymied.

Now, what?

Then a faint feeling at my center begins to stimulate what I realize remains.

The feeling intensifies.

The hardness I feel is coming to attention and shaking, hitting all the receivers located in my now re-warming core.

The vibration is waking all that was ignited and then disappointed.

I shiver.

I shake.

My core re-heats and the vibration intensifies and begins a staccato beat.

My liquid begins to flow again.

My nipples stiffen.

I buck as the vibration pulses hard and insistent.

I lift my hips trying to lean into whatever might send me riding an edge between warmth of here and the forever bliss of exploding heat pushed beyond.

But before I exit, the vibration stops, and the cliff abruptly disappears.

I am left hanging, bucking, trying to catch the ride which has vanished once more.

My skin is heated, lined with moisture which in the sudden absence leaves me cold as moisture evaporates.

I growl in frustration and pull at my bindings.

Still splayed.

Still stymied.

Still frustrated.

I scream, "Make me come, you bastard, make me come!"

I hear feet pad back into the room.

The tension on my right leg relaxes and a hand lifts my leg.

I feel a strap slide under my knee.

Hands release and my leg is suspended.

Now the left leg is released and then strapped at the knee.

Both knees in the air leaving me even more open and displayed.

A finger lightly brushes my clit and I jump.

Breath blows across the entire length of my pussy.

Fingers slip into my opening and gently tease, tugging in and out. More breath.

A tongue lightly edges my clit.

I feel myself getting excited again.

But I'm worried, concerned about a repeat of nothing.

However, this tongue forges on, exploring, tasting, tempting, trying me out.

Seeing what I react to, what makes me jump.

I begin to release my concern, focusing on the exploration, re-heated desire entirely delicious.

The tongue begins to explore more, methodically visiting each crevice, tasting here and there.

Maybe sensing my relaxation and obvious excitement, I feel a mouth sucking not only my clit but a wonderful hard tongue dips inside of me, nudging, pushing.

Then the mouth moves back. Something hard and cool is pushed into my pussy.

Next, I feel a finger, cool with liquid wetness slowly push into my rosebud and pull out.

Now the cool hardness is pulled from my pussy and the much larger tip is gently pushed into my rosebud.

So tight at first until I feel my body relax and accept the long length.

A tongue returns, sucking my clit, exploring and licking.

Like I am a meal to be consumed.

The rhythm building, the intensity increasing.

I've never had anyone so attentive, so insistent.

I feel myself liquefying.

I lose track, becoming so ensnared by this mouth, this tongue.

Oh, God!

Now teeth pulling and nipping.

Tongue pushing inside then returning to my clit, patiently and insistently pushing me over the cliff as I come hard and fast.

A pause.

Then tongue and mouth return, sucking, licking, nibbling on all my parts.

Then this luscious mouth doubles down on my clit, sucking even harder, finger inserted.

I come once more, so fiercely my hips lift up into that insistent month which pulls on me again.

I explode again.

I can barely think.

I feel deliciously spent.

The cock in my ass begins to move … slowly.

Like the train is waiting for me to catch up before pulling out of the station.

A different heat begins to build as the width of the motion asks me to dig even deeper.

The slowness is dragging me though I feel my momentum return and begin to gather.

Each push is deeper and harder.

Each push beyond.

Now the speed is increasing and I can feel the weight of the body bumping me with delicious force.

I have never taken anything to this level.

I have never been taken to this level.

All that has been is gathered again in this moment.

The gathering is tightening all of my core.

The gathering is sending out its own messages.

A low buzz that tightens and expands.

The luscious cock buried in me now ... and now ... and now.

Like all scales there comes a tipping point.

And between this push and that pull, then that shove, I hit the top of the ride and hit free fall, coasting in the light created by the resistance of the tracks.

And then there is no holding back.

A full release that hugs me in and sends me soaring beyond.

I'm wracked with an incredible orgasm ... beyond words, filled with feeling and the emotion of the day.

As I soak into the wave, I realize the voice echoing against the walls is my scream.

And then I hear no more, wrapped in the bliss of the moment.

Nothing needed just the extension of life's powerful forces reverberating within.

———

ONE BY ONE THE STRAPS BEHIND MY KNEES RELEASE AND disappear.

My wrists are released and the straps disappear.

I feel someone stretch out beside me,

A familiar voice says, "Hey baby."

The blindfold lifts and I look into the eyes of my lover, my husband, my best friend.

He smiles, "Happy Birthday, Sweetheart!"

MY LEAD

THE FEMININE

I SLOWLY TIP MY HEAD UP TO GAZE DIRECTLY INTO THE MOST luscious brown eyes.

I smile, lazily, inviting.

His breath catches and his focus narrows, heated.

I let my gaze go.

Looking down, I inhale slowly, biting my lip.

As I inhale again, I look up to find his gaze locked on me.

I feel his heart open.

I reach out with finger tips to trace his heart's door now open for me.

My hand to his chest.

This breath connects me head to toe.

We deliberately open the way for the Goddess who is me to run like sap through my veins.

He feels my/her emergence as a delicious warming tickle on his skin.

The Hunter in him is beckoned forward.

Each in our strength, anticipating, yet open to whatever will be.

I reach for his hand and gently tug him down with me and the pillows and the silky red carpet where I lie.

I slowly run my finger down the bridge of his nose and trace the slope of each lip.

Moving in close, I lightly blow on his ear and then ever more lightly trace his ear with my tongue.

Again, his breath catches.

I can feel him warring inside: lie quietly or move quickly?

I let my finger drop from his chin and trace a line to the center of him.

With a gentle poke, I tell him that in this moment the lead is mine.

I smile and nudge his chin with my nose, and he groans his relent.

Thinking of our very first, and wanting to ignite him now as then, my nose leads my lips to his.

Quietly, gently, I offer a slow, deep kiss.

The warmth gathers and his motion to push forward melts as his arms pull me in.

Down deep I can feel another boil in me begin to gather.

Yet I am not distracted.

Even more fervently, I kiss him again.

He thinks he knows where I'm headed.

I bite his lip and pull.

My finger retraces his nose.

Turning his head slightly, I gently kiss his ear and trail my finger down his neck, kissing his collarbone.

My finger traces the warmth flowing down his arm.

I straddle his chest and slowly slide down until his core and mine are firmly grounded in the heavenly flow of this man, this woman, now.

I settle my opening at just the tip of his pulsing cock.

No further.

His heart beats stronger.

His breath rushes to expand and contract.

My core feels liquid and his eyes are on fire.

Hunter though he is, he has willingly followed.

Asserting my desire, I have willingly led.

I bury myself in his lips and slide his hardness deeply into me, clenching, claiming.

I whisper in his ear, "Honey, it's your lead now! I relent."

———

THE MASCULINE

"Damn!"

I am torn.

Her willingness to lead always pulls at my heart.

Feeling safe with me, pushing her to push me.

My tongue finds her lips.

I nip as gently as I can … though raised heat is tipping me into the bliss of mindlessness.

I want to take her with me.

I sit up and sink my tongue into her mouth.

Gently I roll forward.

Keeping her tight to me, my cock pushing in deeper.

I lay her on the floor and bring her legs against my chest, her heels resting against my shoulders.

She has her preferences.

This is mine.

I can see her eyes.

I can push my cock into her depths, massaging her cervix, pinning her down.

She's so flexible, so willing.

Her eyes are full of heat.

Her skin warm and flushed.

I feel my own heat flare.

I draw almost out and smile at her.

She's gasping, unprepared for that quick withdraw.

She lifts up, rolling back, eyes closing.

That won't do!

"Babe, open your eyes. Look at me!"

She slightly lifts her head and catches my stare.

A slight smile across her lips.

Then I let go and slam in as I watch her catch her breath in surprise.

She opens even more to me and my thrusts.

Her wet heat inflames me further.

I feel myself hurtling us into the abyss.

The next thrust takes us over the edge.

She bucks into me and I meet her fully engorged.

Eyes locked, mouths screaming.

Bodies in full release as we soar.

GOD, GODDESS, AND THE TREES

CIRCLE OPENED

A TWO-DAY HIKE INTO THE BACK COUNTRY.

On the third day, we find the circle.

A ring of magnificent, old-growth cedar trees and, at the center, an open space maybe 40-feet in diameter filled with deep green moss across the forest floor.

I choose our camping spot about two hundred feet away, towards a cliff overlooking the ancient valley below.

The circle doesn't quite make sense geographically, but it is incredibly beautiful.

Plus, I feel such a strong urge to bring her here that I let my intellectual questions slide way.

Besides intellect is not what draws me – or her – here.

Hard to put to words.

But if I make an attempt, I'd say we are here to shift the foundation of ourselves and claim a promise for the future of our relationship.

I met Sophia several months ago in a coffee shop.

Curled up on the window seat of the shop's bay window, she was engrossed in reading.

On the large wooden table in front of her was a tall stack of more books.

In her hand was a rather worn volume, which, as she turned a page, I caught a glimpse of the title.

One of my favorites: *Man's Search for Meaning* by Victor Frankl.

Deep in my observation, I realized she had caught me looking at her.

I remember her open grin as she observed me in return.

"May I join you?" I ask. "You're reading one of my favorites."

She carefully places her bookmark and lays the book on the table next to the other books.

She takes me in again and I become even more aware of her amazing deep brown eyes.

Almost like she is reading my mine, I watch a question form in her mind.

"Do you believe the eyes are windows to the soul?" she asks.

I feel myself take a quick breath, a little surprised, yet very pleasantly enticed because her voice poses the question both quietly and seriously.

There are a million places I can begin. Looking at her, I decide straight forward is best.

She seems to be someone who will prefer honesty over arrogant BS.

Though her eyes are enough to distract me from any intelligible answer.

I take a deep breath and jump in deep.

"I believe our eyes are conduits between the depths of our beings and the depths of all they survey. More than a bridge, eyes receive and translate, yet are also capable of exchange and communication."

I feel a bit like I am defending a thesis before a committee of one.

She smiles, full, open, from the depths of her being, looking both surprised and delighted.

As I look back, I know this was the moment our relationship began.

I WATCH HER MOUTH OPEN, HER TONGUE LIGHTLY RUNNING across her lips as she bites her bottom lip.

As she considers her response, I feel myself pulled into her and her world almost as if I am being submerged into a broad circle of awareness.

She continues, "I like how you acknowledge the flow of our eyes. Most seem to think the eyes are one-way, giving lip-service to the motion of the soul." All the while very intently observing me.

For me, watching her talk lights me from within and I don't mean in just a physical or sexual sense -- though both are happening.

The sensation was like a door that I have always known was there has finally opened.

In the opening out tumbled these incredibly deep parts of myself, no longer locked away, though a bit dusty from a lack of use, yet eager for the deep connection which instinctively my soul's wisdom knew she was offering.

I take a breath and respond, "But isn't that what Frankl is speaking to? That in our quest for meaning, each of us are exploring an ebb and flow which transcends and connects. Don't' eyes stand at the crossroads between the physical and the spiritual, not only able to navigate both worlds, but to also bring them together?"

She leans forward, placing her elbows on the table, hands holding her chin.

"Let me ask you, then, a very important question?"

I nod yes and feel every part of my body tighten in anticipation.

"Coffee or tea?"

Not what I expected but without missing a beat, I answer.

"Coffee in the morning. Tea at night."

"Awesome! Why don't you get some and join me?"

I DID. I JOINED HER AND WE TALKED, LITERALLY ABOUT everything.

Until the cafe closed.

We have been exploring relationship ever since.

Now here we are, together in the forest.

She is trusting me because she has never backpacked before.

I am excited to show her this forest, the trees, and this circle of ancient energy.

My first time here, the forest showed me the possibility of what I could be and become, what I could initiate.

The circle shifted me, extricating me from layers of denial and refusal.

Stripped me to the bone so to speak

I came to see what an arrogant ass I had been.

Stuck in my brain, ignoring the powerful awareness I had of my world, especially of the natural world.

Since then, I have read of others' stories of release and enlightenment.

I know some would say I got in touch with my feminine side.

But I feel it differently.

More like my masculine side quit being so defensive and egotistical.

Instead, this very male part of me came to peace with the feminine aspects of not just myself, but of everything.

Hard to explain except to say that the inner and outer battles are gone.

I am who I am and don't feel like I need to do anything to prove my value.

Since then I have experienced my life more deeply and with greater satisfaction.

Considered highly successful in my field, though now what is most important to me is what I consider an integrated experience on all levels body, mind, heart and soul.

As we talk and have gotten to know each other, I realize it is this integration which she touches.

She has made clear she really likes this integrated part, though also telling me she finds all of me incredibly sexy.

Our relationship has so many moving parts and has evolved quickly and to a depth we are both surprised, yet willing to experience and explore.

While Sophia rests a bit after our post-hike lunch, I turn from our camp and approach the circle.

I STAND IN BETWEEN THE TWO TREES I HAVE IDENTIFIED AS the door.

The space between the trees is almost like an eye because it feels intent on sharing an ebb and flow.

I step through and feel transported out of time.

I see the forest around and the trunks of the thirteen trees which make the circle.

But there is an otherworldly feel which gives me goosebumps.

The trees are so large that the bases of each tree are less than five feet away from each other.

Yet, I feel solidly grounded.

As I've mention, my previous experience here shifted me.

Back then, when I stepped from the circle, my senses were turned up, my awareness seemed to rise above physical boundaries.

I could hear the entire forest from this one point, immediately able to identify creeks and hills, rivers and mountains.

I instinctively knew where the mountain lions, bear, elk, and deer roamed.

From any point of view, I saw and felt the entirety.

I knew I could move freely without worry.

A life-long love of archery, with this new awareness, I was able to track anything quickly and accurately.

However, the most surprising was the activity of the wolves around me.

They sat with me around my campfire, stalked with me in the forest, like I was one of the pack.

The alpha male always sits at my side.

We are two leaders in council with each other and the rest of the group.

Early in our relationship, I decided I needed to be very open with Sophia about this aspect of myself.

If she thought I was crazy, we both needed to know earlier than later.

Sophia listened intently to my story, her eyes never wavering, no indication that she was surprised or repulsed.

Instead, she was the one who explained what had happened.

"You, too, are wolf. The circle initialed you, bringing to the fore your essential energy as the Hunter, you as Horned God. The wolves recognize and respect you as a fellow hunter. The alpha has accepted you as peer."

Wow! This woman is amazing!

Instantly, I knew we needed to make the trek.

If only for her to see the circle and, perhaps, my wolves.

CIRCLE CLAIMED

My mind returns to the present.

I move to the center of the circle to spread a blanket.

The moss cushions each step and I feel the trees nod their agreement.

From my backpack, I retrieve a cloth bundle of rose petals and spread them across the blanket.

Eyes closed, I ask if there was anything else.

From the forest breeze I receive one word, "she" plus a vision of what Sophia and I will experience together in this place.

Returning to our camp, I find Sophia looking at the horizon.

Her back to me, I take a moment to savor the view.

Her light brown hair flutters in the breeze and she has on a hiking skirt which shows off her muscled legs, her gorgeous ass, and curvy, luscious hips.

She is a woman of substance, able to arouse me with just a grin or a light kiss.

Her voice trills tension in me and when her eyes light up, I am transported into a space where all I can see is her.

Where all I want is her.

I walk up behind her and set my hands on her hips, whispering in her ear.

"Are you ready? "I ask. "The circle calls – I want you to see."

"Yes, sweet man – I can't wait!"

She turns in my arms and kisses me lightly.

As I hug her tighter, our kiss deepens.

My hands grasp her butt and I pull her toward me as my cock tightens.

She makes that sound which strikes me as both kitten and lion, but which I now know is a sound I've heard among the wolves.

I take her hand and we set out, both enjoying the layers of forest around us.

While the magnificent trees occupy the scene, tiny details like salal patches, a nurse log covered in moss, tiny white fairy flowers, birdsong, and a lazy butterfly seem to excite and amuse her.

The fragrance of conifer, cool breeze, and ancient soil fill us both with a sense of peace and balance.

We step up to the tree door.

She steps back to survey the scene before her, closes her eyes, and takes a deep breath.

I'm overcome again by her beauty and a fragility anchored within incredible strength.

The touch of her hand on me ignites connection.

Sight, sound, touch, taste, and smell resonate within our shared connection.

Opening her eyes, she looks at me directly, smile on her face.

"I'm ready."

Relieved, I step to her, hugging her once again.

I look into her eyes and feel my world full to overflowing.

I know we are meant to be here now.

I feel her agreement and eagerness for the next steps of our shared path.

"Remember I explained the first steps, but that after that, I'm not certain?"

She nods yes.

At the circle's door, I turn and kiss her, deeply without reserve and she responds in kind.

Reaching for the edges of her shirt, she raises her arms and allows me to remove it for her.

She responds in kind for me.

Next our shoes and socks.

Then my pants and her skirt, then our underwear including her lacey red sports bra.

Piece by piece, each helping the other in a steady, uninhibited flow.

I hug her to me as a forest breeze lightly caresses us both.

Taking her hand, we step just to the threshold.

She gasps, her hold on my hand tightens.

I feel her wobble, seeking to recover her balance.

"Oh, my! I didn't expect such a beautiful sense of power. Like whatever was no longer needed was lifted."

She takes a deep breath to steady herself, and then continues, "Sweetheart, thank you for sharing this with me."

She lifts up on her toes and lightly kisses my lips.

I squeeze her hand and smile at her, my signal to begin.

She lifts her head to take in the circled cathedral of trees and calls out in a clear voice.

"I am ready to take this journey wherever our path may lead."

I feel the trees nod their agreement.

Another hand squeeze and we step over the seemingly invisible line of the door.

She gasps again, and I see tears of pleasure and happiness gather in her eyes.

I realize she feels what I have felt here: a peace and quiet, infused with otherworldly beauty and strength.

A place out of time, time without place.

Without another cue from me, Sophia says to the circle, "I'm here to be guided, to learn, to explore, and open the gates of my essential nature."

Then she turns to me and I see a smile and tears of happiness running down her cheeks.

She looks me square in the eye and continues, "With you, I take this journey because my heart is clear. You are my hunter, my wolf, and my Horned God."

My heart catches as she speaks.

I feel huge joy especially with her last sentence, an addition she chose to make.

I look her in the eye, returning my respect, and declare, "I am here as guide and fellow traveler on a journey with unknown paths. May my hunter and wolf provide you safe space. May my Horned God reflect clear vision of who your Goddess is and can become."

We walk to the center of the blanket, our feet sinking into rose petals and the moss below.

Standing front to front, holding her hands in mine, each of us taking a deep breath, we close our eyes ready to begin the special breathing exercise the circle taught me last time and that we have practiced together.

First, feeling the trees and the ground below, we breath in, feeling the energy of the Earth come up through the soles of our feet and flow into the center of our beings.

Then as we breath out, we bring in the energy of the heavens down through the top of our head, and into the center of being.

Breath in and out, feeling heaven and earth meet and balance at center.

With each inhale and each exhale, we come to balance between heaven and earth.

Soon I feel her squeeze my hand, and without opening my eyes, I pull her into my arms, breath in sync, balance with and between.

This time I do not hold back.

I find her lips and let my feelings go completely into my mouth on hers, tongues intertwining, bodies pressed.

Her arms wrap around me and pull me even closer.

I feel the hardness of her nipples smashed against me.

I know she feels the hardness of my cock.

As I draw my next breath, I feel a presence emerge and, in my vision, I see a beautiful woman standing within the circle, several feet away from us behind Sophia.

She is naked but adorned with flowers and vines which form a crown at her head and then weave through her hair to fall beyond her hips.

Her beauty is exhilarating and voluptuous – just like Sophia.

The circle is filled with the melodious whisper of this otherworldly feminine presence.

"I am the Goddess of the Wild Hunt. Welcome to my altar."

Sophia startles.

Then we both hear a masculine, throaty whisper here behind me and I know Sophia both sees and hears him.

"I am the consort of the Goddess, the Horned God, the Hunter."

The Goddess begins to walk clockwise around us, and by the move of his voice, the Hunter joins the path.

The Hunter comes into my vision.

He is tall and muscular, naked with a bow slung across his back.

He looks as hard as I feel.

Beyond my initial instructions, we have now moved to the part of the journey unknown to me.

"Dear ones," the Goddess begins. "You are here to receive our blessing and make the Wild Hunt part of your journey."

"This is a sacred path," the Hunter continues. "A path which requires a willingness to always step into the unknown.

"For this is the Wild Hunt. A journey of passion guided by deeply connected hearts," chants the Goddess.

The Hunter stops within my view and looks me in the eye.

"The first choice comes from you. Are you willing to offer space to her? Willing to risk her rejection?"

I look into Sophia's beautiful eyes and feel no doubt.

"Yes, always!" I promise.

The Goddess now behind me softly inquires, "And you, dear girl, are you willing to take your own risk? Are you willing to receive what he offers? Are you willing to be the crucible of truth for this relationship?"

I look at Sophia as she tips her head to look at me.

A sweet smile crosses her face. "Yes, always!'

"Lovely!" the Goddess responds.

"You are here because we believe you ready. You have already taken the first steps. You are both open to the other. You are learners both of self and of other."

The Hunter joining the Goddess, both standing behind me.

He asks me, "Son, I believe you now know what to do. She is for you to trust, to protect, and to recognize and support the truth of her existence. If you don't offer, she has nothing to receive."

Following on his words, the Goddess continues, "Daughter-mine, this man is also for you to trust and protect. It's your capacity which transforms the relationship. In offering your vulnerability, you create the space for him to transform into your equal."

They stand for a moment, perhaps giving us time to reflect.

"In the Wild Hunt," the Goddess begins.

The Hunter continues, "The role of the Hunter is to give the Goddess sacred space to come undone, to let go."

"Look, my boy," the Hunter advises. "If you don't truthfully demonstrate that she can trust you, then she will be left fending for herself, lost in the strength she has developed as protection from a world in which it is very challenging for her to be both beautiful and smart."

"And Daughter-mine," the Goddess adds. "When you trust your Hunter, you realize you can lay your shield down in his presence. This allows you freedom to go beyond any inner limitation. Your receiving of what he offers allows him the space to experience vulnerable grace and allows you to bring forward what he can receive. He offers, you receive. Then you offer, he receives."

"Sounds simple, doesn't it?" the Hunter inquires, a mischievous grin on his face.

"But nothing can be between you two unless you both are open and ready to learn about yourself, each other, and all the world has to offer."

The Hunter has come full circle again and embraces his Goddess.

They look at each other the way I feel Sophia and I look at each other.

The Hunter turns towards me and whispers in my ear. "Son, you've got the best. Don't screw up! And for Goddess's sake, don't be a push-over. She likes you cuz you got the balls to stand up to her. Don't disappoint. Remember, it's all about the delicious tension. Keep that going and you're golden."

He squeezes my shoulder and winks.

I notice the Goddess stepping back from Sophia.

Sophia whispers loudly to the Goddess, "Thank you for your advice! I agree. The edge is both frightening and exhilarating but the only place where intimacy and depth emerge."

I feel them embrace each other.

"All right sugars," the Goddess calls. "The next step is all yours. If you say yes, then you will call down the Wild Hunt and each of you will emerge as the Hunter or Goddess you each can claim from the truth of who you are. It's a wild, beautiful ride!"

"Enjoy!" the Hunter calls. "We will leave you two alone even though from this day forward we will be with you always."

We watch them walk through the threshold of the circle. The Hunter pats the Goddess' behind as she steps into the circle of his arms.

Ready to begin but feeling a bit shy, I turn to Sophia and smile.

She lifts her hand to mine and says, "Show me how."

I pull her close and kiss her deeply, feeling myself harden yet more.

I've never felt so certain of anything.

I sink to my knees, bringing her with me.

"Breathe," I ask. "Breathe with me. Let us find our balance first."

Face to face, we begin.

Her hands cup my face and she lightly kisses my lips.

Her fingers trace my jaw and she snuggles into me, her head below my chin.

Laying down on the blanket, I pull her under me, again feeling her tenderness and her strength.

We kiss deeply, and I know the time to begin has come.

I move my mouth to her breast and gently suck her nipple.

Then to the other, gently taking her into my mouth and then insistently tugging, hoping for a reaction.

She responds in a groan and whispers, "More!"

Empowered, I slide further down, and my tongue finds her clit, engorged, wet, ready.

Silently to myself, encouraged by the Hunter, I vow to take her further.

I suck on her hard button, licking, sucking, slightly pulling.

She squirms and groans for more.

My finger slips into her pussy and begins to rub the spongy entrance.

Slowly I increase the pressure and the rhythm, feeling a wave of release hit her again.

I watch her buck in response.

I return my mouth to her clit and continue to explore her pussy now with two fingers.

Watching her response, watching her trust me in her release gives me such joy felt in every cell of my body.

She tenses just a moment and then unable to resist, the tide rolls across again.

I hold her as the last wave rockets through.

She looks into my eyes and smiles reflecting her own satisfaction and her own joy.

Pushing me to my back, she straddles me and bends to kiss me deeply. Oh, God!

She scoots down my body and finds my cock with her warm mouth.

We've done this all many times before.

But in this moment, in this place, all before pales in comparison.

She knows exactly what turns me on and she licks my tip, pushing her tongue into the small slit, then around the hard ridge.

Now down my shaft, first lightly and then with more pressure.

Until.... again, oh my God!

She takes me entirely into her mouth in one motion, allowing the end of my cock to graze the back of her throat.

She has centered me, all of me into one point of shared attention.

Her wet, warm mouth around my hard, hard cock.

Very slowly she is moving her mouth back and forth along the length of my shaft.

Licking and sucking, nailing me.

I run my fingers through her hair, enjoying the sensation of my hands in her hair and her mouth lightly blowing my pubic hair as her tongue and mouth work their magic.

I feel my Hunter step forward.

I feel her Goddess respond.

I pull her up to kiss and we roll over, me on top feeling the power and softness of her lovely body.

Soft skin, curves, pillowy breasts which fill my hands.

My knees sink between her legs and I shift to kneeling between her spread legs.

I gaze into the eyes of the most beautiful woman, cheeks rosy with excitement, lips puffed ready for me, for more.

"Ready?" I ask.

"Yes! All of you! Now!" she whispers as a groan cuts off her words.

I bring my cock to her center knowing that in this motion now I am changing our lives forever.

I am ready to offer, and she is ready to receive.

I insert a finger from each hand into her pussy, pulling her gently wider.

She is so wet!

My cock finds her opening and I slowly enter watching her eyes, observing the motion of response in her body.

I feel her take me in.

I feel her open.

I feel myself receive her offering.

The motion takes me into the deepest feeling of love I have ever felt.

She arches up, offering all her, legs opening wide then digging into my back to bring me into her deeper.

Heat sizzling along every edge where skin meets skin.

I feel consumed.

I feel us connect within and without.

No end.

No beginning.

Just now.

Time suspended.

Space is but her and me.

But then I feel a breeze from the trees, from the circle.

She feels the same because her eyes open in amazement trying to see if I feel it, too.

The rose petals dance around us and the earth's deep, mossy scent fills our noses.

Sunlight dances through the trees, casting both shadow and light across us.

I feel myself balanced between Heaven and Earth, with Sophia, we are connected center to center, our individual beings becoming our joined awareness.

In my awareness, I feel that she has the same sense of balance and connection.

I begin to move my cock with greater rhythm and more intense push.

I feel her legs lift and embrace me again, her hands clasping my back, pulling me in, deeper, longer, harder.

Now as my motion increases, I feel her first wave of orgasm.

I slow a bit to let her ride the waves.

Watching as her eyes close and she surfs the flow of her and me within.

I keep moving, my cock sinking deeply into her as another wave explodes across the beauty of her body.

Now the energy of my Hunter is throbbing through my cock, calling to her Goddess.

A familiar voice comes with overtones of the Goddess and Sophia screams, "I am Goddess and I call the Wild Hunt!"

Another wave hits her, and she crests the flow.

Then her eyes beckon mine.

"I call you forth my Hunter, you are mine."

The largest energy surge I have ever felt rips through every bit of me.

Cock submerged in crucible ignites us both.

A flame turns to raging fire.

The edge beckons.

The edge pulls.

Nothing to do but let go, let come – whatever maybe.

We feel the energy of everywhere and nowhere explode through us with unexpected force.

She comes.

I come.

More waves of power and joy.

But we are not done.

We dare the edge and make the vulnerable choice of free fall.

My heart is ripped from my body.

I offer all that I am to Sophia, freely, without reservation.

Our bodies focused yet beyond rational control, seeking euphoria, understanding it's not about taking but about offering and receiving.

Her and me beyond individual definition.

Thrusting into the edges which push us into the love of the mutual hunt.

I yield and I accept.

She, too, yields and accepts.

Her body lifts into mine, reciprocating on every level of my offering.

She looks at me, fusing her awareness with mine.

I rub her nipples in my fingers, capturing her body in every way that I can.

Tears streak her face.

I tug harder as she bucks again under me.

Her body is glowing, radiating the heat I have raised up in her.

As I feel her pull me into her, I tremble feeling the ecstatic waves rise within her like the Goddess that she is.

She smiles and we are caught in a still moment between what will be and what will never be again.

The threshold opens, the edge rips, and we are pushed together to fall into the unknown of release.

My cock claiming her opening, I release fully, filling her as she screams.

I come again feeling the waves hit her shore with the intensity of a euphoric hurricane pounding away the past, leaping into the future of who we be together.

I yield and collapse.

She draws me into her arms.

We, both, spent.

We, both, consumed.

We, both, edged.

Time passes, but my awareness is for her only.

I pull her into my arms, lightly caressing her body, giving her space to be, to hopefully not feel any need to do.

My awareness begins to open to the circle.

I feel the sheltering trees and as I look around, surprise catches my breath.

On the outside of the circle, facing away from us, a wolf sits between each tree as sentry, as guard.

"Sophia, baby, we are not alone."

She looks, taking in the scene, then looks at me with wonder and awe.

I give her a light kiss and whisper in her ear, "You are my Goddess!"

She kisses me in return, then whispers, "You are my Hunter."

Together we are a completed circuit of masculine and feminine, safe within the offer and acceptance.

Here in the forest and the trees.

God and Goddess.

Willing always to create the wild hunt together.

UNLIMITED HEAT

SITTING ON HIS LAP, HIS WARM BREATH BLOWS GENTLY ACROSS my ear.

I shiver, moistened.

I feel my ear lean in asking for tongue.

A flick on my lobe, a soft swish across, followed by more breath, blowing lightly top to bottom.

Then his tip reaches into my ear's center and I shudder in remembrance and in anticipation.

He pulls back slightly, running tongue across his lip, thoughtful, considering his next step.

I jump as a finger lightly touches the back of my neck and begins to slowly, lightly trace the line of my spine.

Now my back leans in, adjusting, shifting into a different direction, trying to catch the finger and press against its motion down.

I shudder involuntarily as his finger ignites my centers of feeling and deepening sensation.

About halfway down, his finger stops and drills in.

I am unable to focus except on that delicious pressing point on my back.

As he shifts in his seat, I feel the rise of his breath aiming once again at my ear.

My center lights and the tips of my breasts explode in tingling sensation, unable to wait.

I shudder again and shift in my body as fire lights.

I sigh.

He leans in and whispers, "Can I come in?"

Reason fades as sensation and fire respond.

Before I answer, another finger gently caresses my other ear and draws down a spark to shoulder and arm, gently tracing to my finger's end.

I do not want to speak, instead I respond.

I turn toward his mouth and, with my tongue, lightly trace his lips.

The finger in my back presses in more, pushing me in closer, my tongue now tracing just inside his mouth.

My finger moves slowly towards his chin, to steady, to anchor, to hold him ready for the motion of my finger across his cheek and into his ear.

My center is on fire.

Yet all I care to do is take gentle steps to strike his match.

His finger is still, pressing into my back.

I shudder each time he presses in.

From every point comes wet heat and fire.

Now his finger drops, continuing a journey to the end.

At the in-between, he stops and once again presses, this time between the cheeks of my ass.

No longer sitting, he is rising and brings me face to face.

This motion allows me to take my own step.

I turn 180 degrees, slowly, allowing his finger and his breath to trace my trail.

He shudders, he growls.

I stop, my back to his front.

Slowly I reach my hands up and lift my hair.

Slightly tipping my head, I offer my neck.

Now his breath returns with moisture and heat, quickly expelled across my bare skin.

His lips suck and his teeth nip.

I shudder, I groan.

My knees almost buckle.

Two strong hands settle to each side of my waist, pulling me in, unable to miss the return of his tongue, barely grazing my neck.

His tongue wets me all over as it explores from bottom to top, side to side, igniting and tingling every nerve in my body.

His finger returns to the middle of my back, finding blade to trace and caress.

I can't help myself.

I respond with a sigh and a shake.

His finger continues down my spine and slowly presses the same deliciously low spot.

At the same time, his other hand shifts gently to the center of my chest and his finger traces the same line, stopping in front at the same point as his finger in my back.

I feel caught on a line from front to back, pulling and pressing.

All feeling is ignited, pulsing with heat.

Sensing my need, he pulls me into his chest, tenderly biting my neck.

I can't stop as my center explodes, melting my resolve to take him with me.

I can barely stand except that I am completely pressed in and now feeling him shake.

Tempo gathers.

I turn in his arms, finding his lips with my tongue.

I pull him tight, tracing my finger very firmly along the line of his spine until I feel him jump.

A growl erupts around my tongue and we find the wall.

His hands grab mine and he lifts my arms above my head pinning me.

I can tell no more sighs, no more slow, no more show.

His knee slides between both of mine.

He presses in with mouth and breath bringing more moisture and heat.

Now his other knee slides in and lifts me up.

I hang in balance on the brink of hard boil.

His tongue finds the depression in the front of my neck, lingering only a little before its descent.

I shudder.

My center begins a new sizzle as his knee firmly finds purchase at the juncture where everything begins and eventually ends.

Again, his tongue across this collar bone and now that one.

His knee moves firmly and intently, stoking my fire.

Sweet breath across my neck, breasts ripe for a pinch and a pull.

My arms reach up, pushing my chest forward and his tongue quickly teases, and his fingers do more.

I gush.

I whimper.

God, I do want more!

Hands on my butt, he lifts me up and settles me down.

Quickly, his cock claims my wetness and my heat.

I scream out his name.

I shiver, and I shift, and I press in, wanting every inch.

In no apparent hurry, he does not move.

Teasing me, daring me.

Now his finger intently pushes down the frontline of my spine and my arms reach up to gather strength.

His tongue finds a nipple to suck and pull.

His hands find my back side as lever to rotate and press.

The balance tips and, as if I'd actually uttered a yes, he begins to pump me, pinning me to the wall with each eager shove and push.

Me dragging my fingers across his back, leaving trails of moisture and heat.

I open.

I feel.

I scream with delight.

His hardness, my moisture, our heat pinpointing all sensation to a singular focus: only him and his motion and me.

With another stroke, I am no longer aware of what's him or me.

Now only a balance boiling and building.

All I can feel is I want more, longer, faster and harder.

Pushed to the edge, the border, the heat.

Pulled toward the valley of lighted desire.

Held in the moment where two bodies meet.

In the push and the pull comes the delicious, the complete.

A shudder.

A scream.

A release in the push-me-pull-you connection of two bodies joined in unlimited heat.

BIT HARD

He sits on the sofa, slowly tracing his lip.

Lightly across the top and then firmly across the bottom.

Pulling a bit just as she did to him last night with her lips and teeth.

Lost in the memory, he feels his hands reach out and run his fingers down the softness of her arms.

Her elbows bending to reach fingers to his face and softly cup his chin.

Lifting his head, he sees her eyes fill with anticipation and a soft grin spreads across the beauty of her face.

A view which always draws wonders and joy within.

Reaching to touch her face, he feels her step closer, bending towards him.

Her lips find his cheek and tenderly brush a kiss.

Her hand slowly traces the outer ridge of his right ear.

Her grin becomes pursed lips, blowing lightly across the ridge of his cheekbone.

Lips follow her hand.

Her tongue traces the ridge of his earlobe.

The tip sinks into the depths of his ear, lightly lapping, warming with liquid heat.

He feels himself harden and any urge to stop fades.

UNWILLINGLY, THE SOUND OF THE TELEVISION INTRUDES.

He is abruptly jerked out of his reverie into his surroundings … though the feel of her tongue lingers.

In fact, more lingers.

He brings a pillow onto his lap to hide the effect of remembering her.

Despite his schooling to keep strict hold on himself, he smiles, finding deep satisfaction in his memory of her realness.

Refocusing on the screen in front of him, the memory of her touch remains.

A precious awareness.

As he has done before, he knows if he allows himself, he can bring her fully to life in this moment.

But right now, with others around, he knows he shouldn't.

Instead, he contents himself with the inner awareness of her tongue just before it sinks into his ear.

———

"HEY, JEFF! HOW'S THE GAME GOING?"

His friend Tom returns from the kitchen with beers for them both.

Sunday afternoons he and his friends gather for conversation and football.

He is not a committed fan of the game, but he likes the gathering.

"Hey, thanks! Nothing has happened," Jeff grins, knowing that's not completely true.

Her finger brushes his shoulder as he begins to speak.

As Tom stretches out on the sofa besides Jeff, he says, "I just heard from Aki. He is on his way and bringing BBQ. God, I love that stuff! "

"Hey, how's that new girl? Having fun?" Tom inquires.

Jeff feels himself twitch under the pillow.

Her kiss on his cheek light as a butterfly.

"She's great!" Jeff replies as a finger slides down his chest.

"We had a great time at the concert Friday night."

He gives his friend a big smile.

Tom returns his grin.

"Dude, I'm really happy for you. About time! Tell me more about her. What's she do?"

Tom takes a swig of his beer and gives his best friend an encouraging smile.

"Well, she does a lot. She's a writer like me but she also has her own business which keeps her busy. We seem to have a lot in common. I love the way she listens and, man, her smile..."

Jeff lifts his hands and shoulders, shrugging not knowing exactly how to continue because all he can see are her wickedly luscious lips.

"That's awesome, man. So happy for you! Hope you're enjoying her in other ways."

Tom winks and grins.

"Oh, I am! Believe me! Like I said we are very similar!"

The pillow still necessary as her hand slides down his front resting on the bulge in his pants.

"Awesome! Glad to hear your dry spell is over! That was getting really painful to watch. I get you are picky, but seriously two years is just too much. I know I couldn't do that."

"Well, some things in life are definitely worth waiting for and she is one of those for me."

Her hand begins to gently rub.

"I'm glad you found her! Aki and I were starting to think we were gonna have to step in. And I suspect that while one part of you might have liked what we found, your brain would have been none too pleased. I know you like your girls smart. Not my thing ... but I know you do."

Another voice joins in.

"Hey, Tom, you already grilling Jeff? I don't want to miss out! Whatcha find out already?"

Aki lays a huge bag on the table, a tangy, smoky aroma fills the room.

"Aki, our friend here is more than smitten."

"Oh, really?" grinning Jeff's way.

"Yep! He's been bit and bit hard, if you ask me."

"Excellent! Jeff, man, glad to hear it! What's she look like?"

Jeff looks at his friends and grins.

"Don't laugh ... she's a goddess."

Aki and Tom grin ear to ear and wait.

Jeff doesn't often offer up much.

"She has the most beautiful dark brown eyes. Hair soft and golden. And the cutest little fingers."

"Oh, man!" Aki exclaims. "You're right, Tom, he is bit hard!"

"Guys give me a break!" Jeff pleads.

"Don't worry! We will! We're just happy for you, Jeff!" Aki responds.

"We don't want to get in the way. Long overdue, buddy!"

The guys turn their attention to the game, unloading the contents from the BBQ bag.

Jeff, relieved, joins the conversation even though his memory of her fingers across his skin bubbles just under the surface of his awareness.

As he listens to his friends discuss the game, her fingers return to his waist and slip in under his belt, lightly grazing his tip.

Quickly he must stifle a groan, covering his face with a silly grin.

"Hey, you guys want another beer?" Jeff asked as he stands up and quickly turns away.

Both Tom and Aki shake their heads no as Jeff escapes, heading to the bathroom.

Closing the door behind him, he leans against the wall and grabs a towel.

With a deep breath, he sees her turn a mischievous grin his way as she unbuckles his belt and unzips his pants.

She presses her entire body against his side, mushing her breasts into his chest and several of her luscious fingers encircle the tip of his cock, lightly pulling.

He is rock hard.

He knows she knows.

Her fingers lightly caress his tip, teasing.

He hears her ask, ready?

Her hand gently pumps.

First slowly, then gaining speed and intensity.

Her tongue finds his ear and suddenly he is wet and hot, panting.

She leans into him more, her mouth replacing her hand, pulling out his pleasure.

The towel raises just in time as he comes, oblivious to anything but the feel of her hand and her tongue.

"Oh, man!" Jeff mutters to himself. "I am bit hard!"

———

HAND OF MY HUNTER

OPENING HAND

A COOL BREEZE FROM THE NORTH BLOWS THE DEEP SCENT OF old forest into my awareness.

I am distracted.

The soft bed of needles below my feet, built up over the years, absorb my steps, muffling my progress down the path.

Along both sides of the trail tall Cedar trees reach into the sunny sky above.

The trees are not the distraction.

No, they surround me like silent guardians holding space for the journey.

My distraction is human.

Him.

His hand.

Specifically, his hand on my back.

Ever since I met him and, especially since we began hiking together, he has this way of gently pressing his hand into the center of my low back.

Other guys have done the same but with less grace and intention, and usually in a way which bothered me.

His hand isn't a bother.

Not at all.

His hand is light and firm.

Clearly there, but never in a pestering manner.

He usually touches just for a moment.

A graze.

A reassurance.

Sometimes to communicate the direction, sometimes to indicate he is listening and understands and doesn't want to interrupt.

At other times, his hand encourages me to continue or to take care.

Mostly his hand is a subtle hint of connection.

A simple I'm-here-for-you gesture.

Initially, this type of subtlety endeared him to me.

His ability to turn the touch of his hand into so much, so quickly, so lightly, so insistently.

Able to assert himself without dismissing me.

Neither dominating nor aggressive, rather a calm awareness of what he wants and what he is willing to do to claim his desire.

A balance alluring in its aim at me not as object but as dream fulfilled.

Doesn't really sound like it should be a distraction, does it?

But … well it is and probably will always be.

Delightfully so.

Here's why: Sparkle.

Yes! Sparkle.

Every time his hand touches my back, a sparkle ignites.

Like a neuron jumping the synapse, I feel the energy of him arc across the tiny space between his hand and my back.

Then, as his hand closes in, the energy compresses and just as contact is made, there is ignition.

A sparkle.

The first time his hand touched my back, I was surprised to feel the sizzle.

I decided I had imagined the sparkle.

The second time the sparkle was undeniable.

The third time I felt myself lean into his hand for more.

The fourth time ... well, the fourth time I finally realized that it was also me reaching out to him, anticipating his hand, contributing to the compression, co-creating the sparkle.

His hand on my back, energy sizzles and sails up the inner core of my body, lifting me up.

At the same time, energy also settles down, soaking into the lower center of my core.

Literally stoking my fire.

Every time: Hand. Sparkle. Wow!

I look him in the eye expecting some comment.

Instead I get his smile and, "Hey sugar, you okay?"

"Mmmm...." I begin, but no intelligent words come to mind.

All I can feel is the need for more sparkle.

Coming from a deep place within us both, the sparkle is a wonderful feeling.

But, why is it distracting?

It's all about location.

Sparkle settles in that place within me where heat is ignited and pulls at response.

Sparkle makes me yearn for him to immediately back me up against a tree, sink his tongue into my mouth, and push his knee between my legs, rubbing my core.

Sparkle makes me hope he won't stop there – that he will ignite more.

The sparkle is his promise, a match gently thrown onto the flame of my core.

A subtle nuance which ignites exponentially.

I remember my Moma telling me that there are many wonderful experiences to have while you're young.

However, she opined, there are some experiences which only get better with age and some which need deeper experience to understand fully the depth of possibility.

Sometimes life is in the horizon.

But sometimes life is not big movement, rather subtle nuance.

Like a hand on a low back creating sparkle.

As a teenager, I remember the thrill of holding hands with a guy, the quick first kiss followed by a rough paw furtively snatched away.

Or the horse blanket on my bare butt as we tried sex for the first time in the back of his uncle's 1960 Ford truck.

Fun.

Feeling forbidden fruit.

Sticky and sweet.

But no deep core sparkle because I was too young to know that kind of deep touch was possible.

Then there was the guy I *almost* married.

The first guy to take the time to make me come with luscious tongue.

More fruit to be licked and eaten.

Rainbows shooting.

But more like a rowboat than a yacht.

Got the job done but without much style.

Finally, I moved on.

To this day, I still puzzle over my yes to the guy I married.

Maybe it's simply because he is the one who asked.

He didn't have the youthful pizazz of a 1960s Ford truck.

Nor the skilled tongue of Mr. Rowboat.

Honestly, I think it was not a yes to him – rather a no to me.

At the time I was both intrigued and embarrassed about my growing interest in something more than vanilla sex.

In marriage, my Moma's sage words forgotten, I turned away from exploring that deeper, perhaps kinky, road.

Then I met the Jet-set master on a business trip to Portland.

A meeting just after the soon-ex confessed his two-year affair with his secretary who he apparently turned to for afternoon delight.

That explained the now perfunctory nature of what I had come to think of as robot sex.

Master Jet-set was payback in that I-don't-give-a-shit-just-get-me-off-now kind of way that only the rejected demand.

I will say that he taught me a thing or two about both men and women and the judicious use of red silk ties.

He showed me the difference between the bike path and the deep road into the valley, which actually gains the higher peak.

With him I felt I was no longer floundering in a tiny boat of typical but was taken in a solid, ocean-going ship to the high seas of deep edge.

However, within the hollow enforced casualness of we-are-all-grownups-here, Master Jet-set had no desire to fulfill my longing for the even deeper connection of heart awareness.

Then one day in a coffee shop.

Me sitting in a bay window seat, a table and a stack of books before me.

He – him with the hands – walks in.

I look up into deep brown eyes.

Then coming from who knows where, this unexpected thought blasts into my mind, "Finally, my Hunter has come!"

Covering up my sudden thrill, and weak knees if I had been standing, I give him trouble.

I want to know how he is with witty give and take.

Is his mind connected to his heart?

Can he make my soul come?

This day is also the first time my back became acquainted with his hand.

We sit in the coffee shop all afternoon, rain pouring outside.

Inside warm comfort and heated conversation.

We spar and share increasing levels of spontaneous depth and awesome puns on everything from quantum physics to whether red was the new black.

Him: black will always be the color of the little dress.

Me: a moot point. Red is in its own very special category. Red and black must learn to co-exist.

About 5:30pm the rain lets up and he asks me for dinner.

I almost say no just because, but I am too intrigued.

As we leave the cafe, he opens the door, steps through and to the side to hold the door open for me as I pass.

In this short walk I learn about his hand.

His right hand gently guides me through and to his left towards the restaurant up the street.

Hand. Sparkle.

His hand keeps us connected through crowds on the sidewalk.

Hand. Sparkle. Wow! Huh?

We arrive at the restaurant and again his hand helps us navigate the door.

Hand. Sparkle. More!

After my doubts from the first hand fade, each time, I feel him behind me.

Each time I want to lean back into him, to take his measure, and figure out why the sparkle.

But the fourth time, as we follow the waiter to our table, maybe my defenses are melting away, but this fourth time I am hooked into what can be created between him and me.

Hand.

On me.

Lordy! His sparkle – our sparkle – ignites the deepest of fire.

As I sit down, I'm boiling hot, ready to let go.

More than willing to skip dinner and let him know how wet I am just from his hand.

I pause and compose, afraid that a groan will give me away in the middle of the busy restaurant.

Does my hunter know what he has already captured just with the sparkle of his hand?

Now here we are hiking in the forest, following a now developed pattern.

Me in front where he likes me to be – and where I am very happy to sashay.

We talk, laugh, tell jokes, sing songs, soaking in the mystic and the primal.

His hand occasionally gently on my back, especially when we pause to take in the forest or a scenic vista, stopping to enjoy the view together.

His hand resting on my back, lightly stroking.

Sparkles flaring.

Heat flowing.

Bodies anticipating.

HANDY REQUEST

About two miles into this our first hike, as we move along the trail, he asks, "How do you feel about surprises?"

I stop, turning to gauge the context of his question.

Him: dimpled smile, open, receptive, waiting.

Giving him a smile in return, I answer, "I love surprises, but only if it's a good surprise. Something I like or enjoy."

"Okay, good to know."

I wait for more, but he just smiles at me and on we go.

Another ten minutes, we come to a small waterfall flowing down the hillside and across the path.

Nothing that can't be easily crossed stepping from stone to stone.

His hand to my back indicating he'll go first.

Crossing, he turns to me offering his hand as I step across.

Just as I think I will keep following the path, his hand pulls me towards him and into his arms.

He smiles, eyes lit.

Sparkles like a firework display everywhere his hands are touching.

Pop, sizzle, crackle.

Then his hand behind my neck and his lips find mine.

The other hand cups my butt, pulling me in tight.

His tongue in my mouth ignites heat.

I push back, tongue meeting tongue.

Sparkle from every point of contact.

I'm lost in his mouth, plastered to his warm body.

In that moment, all forgotten except the many points where we touch and sparkle.

Then he pulls back slightly, creating a tiny separation.

Smiling, he says, "Surprise sugar!"

Then leans down for a quick peck with heated lips.

"Unless you want to protest, here's what I propose. Sometimes with warning, but mostly not, I'm gonna surprise you like I just did. Okay?"

I feel the exhilaration of his offer.

He holds me, challenging, asking, taking a chance.

His hands fingering all of my edges.

Yet between the contact, the compression, and the sparkly explosions, there is safety with him, me, us.

Sparkles propelling us together, ready to explore the unknown.

"You mean you want to do this?" I inquire.

I lightly bite his lower lip.

Then I give all of me into the deepest kiss I can muster considering my wobbly knees.

I step into him as tightly as I can manage, intentionally touching all of him with all of me.

Wanting to meld us together where there's nothing but heat and sparkle.

Never enough sparkle.

I step back sending him a mischievous grin.

His breathing rough, his eyes on fire, he replies "Yes, sugar! Exactly!"

"Then bring it on, sweet man!" I loudly whisper in response, feeling my own heat intensify.

His hand to my back and ... damn! Sparkle!

"But with one caveat, ok?" I challenge.

"Of course!"

"I want to surprise you, too. And not just on the trail, " I request.

A slow smile across his face.

"Always!" he replies.

That's been part of our continued fun: anticipating surprise, devising moments to catch each other unaware.

Each time: luscious, delicious, heated sparkle.

Wonderful, sizzling distraction for two.

HANDOVER

The first moment I saw her I felt a primal urge to protect, to be her guide, to entwine my life with hers.

No matter what it takes, like a cougar stalking prey through the forest, I knew I would overcome any obstacle to claim her and be hers.

She didn't make it easy.

She's wicked smart and playful in a manner which demands all of me.

But I love her challenge – her as adventure!

Definitely not the kind of woman who will tolerate half-ass efforts.

With her, all I ever considered was my A-game, dressed to kill.

Our initial meeting was electric and as we moved from coffee shop to restaurant, I got my first up close feeling of her.

As I ushered her out the door, I instinctively placed my hand on her back and felt a pulse, a spark.

Surprisingly, I wasn't surprised because we had already dipped into the easy flow I've always desired.

The spark was the result of the flow telling me that I was on the right track.

She made me feel like alpha male finding his equal mate.

Every chance I get, my hand, her back, intense sparks of connection, reflecting deep attraction.

Now, here we are on one of my favorite hikes.

A long hike with elevation gain spread over eight miles.

She's pleasantly talkative and inquisitive, lit from within, my forever target.

I'm plotting my next surprise.

The consideration heating my blood, lust building.

I know the trail and in another mile is a flat meadow area shielded by a gorgeous stand of Cedar.

The perfect place for surprise.

"Hey, sugar," I begin. "Ready for a short break soon?"

She stops and turns to me, "Sure, sweet man! I'd be glad to stop with you a bit."

I watch her hand come to her mouth and her eyes light up as she blows me a kiss.

In a few more minutes, I see our resting place.

I'm excited because the meadow is filled with wildflowers which I know she will love.

"Sugar, let me show you the way. I hope you like the spot as much as I."

She follows me off the trail and at the edge of the circle of trees surrounding the tiny meadow, I stop and set my backpack against a tree.

Turning to her, I help her with her pack and watch as her eyes light up.

"Such a beautiful spot!" she whispers.

"Want to try something?" I whisper in her ear.

She nods her head.

I take her hand and my other hand goes to her back as I guide her into the center of the meadow.

"Stand right here. Close your eyes and tell me what you hear."

Again, she nods her head yes and closes her eyes.

I take a couple of steps back, marveling at the way the sunlight dances in her hair.

"Birds," she whispers. "I hear the songbirds."

"What else?" I whisper.

She pauses.

I'm holding my breath in anticipation, curious at what she'll pickup.

"Water. I hear running water."

She inhales.

"I smell the ancient spirit of the forest."

I smile knowing her awareness runs deep.

"You," she begins. "I smell your heat."

"Keep your eyes closed just a minute more, please," I ask.

I walk quietly toward her and place my hands on her shoulders.

"Hey, sugar," I begin. "Surprise!"

I lean forward, my mouth reaching for hers, finding wet warmth as our lips touch.

My hands slide around her shoulders and I pull her to me in a complete embrace.

Her mouth meets mine without resistance.

I love her ability to step quickly into the flow.

I feel my body begin the hum which always emerges when I touch her.

Pulling back, I look at her.

Eyes sparkling, an amused smile, toes touching.

"Close your eyes and let me guide you. OK?" I ask.

Without words, she closes her eyes and waits.

I return my hands to her shoulders and gently push her backward.

Trusting me, she steps, one, two, three, four.

Then I slow our motion to gently lay her against the tree trunk of the largest Cedar in the meadow.

"Right where I want you!" I whisper. "Eyes stay closed, please."

I drop to my knees and gently rub my head into her center where legs join torso.

Running my hands up and down her legs, I feel her shiver, I feel her tremble.

Standing up, I run my hands inside her shirt feeling her warm skin which I've been thinking about the entire hike.

No matter the temperature, her skin always has this amazing soft warmness which heats me.

Though she can definitely overheat me, running my hands over skin brings a pleasant buzz.

I feel myself lose awareness of anything but her and her skin and her willingness to allow me in.

I revisit those lips, sucking them into my mouth, teeth grazing and pulling.

I feel my cock expanding, quickening, hardening.

As good as it might be to nail her here, now, I focus on the sensation of her skin, her lips, her hips pressed to mine.

I want to know every level of her.

I want her to unfold for me.

A bloom only I see and experience.

Now her hands reach under my shirt, sparks flying as she slowly feels me.

She presses to my lips more insistently.

I return her motion with my own and move one leg between hers, gently lifting knee to rub her pussy.

Her hands slip behind me and into my pants.

I almost lose it as she grabs my butt cheeks, fingernails scraping across skin.

I move my hands to do the same to her.

Holding on, I lean away to look her in the eyes.

"You are beautiful." I whisper.

"You make my heart sing," she returns.

I crush her lips and extend my tongue, drinking the elixir that is her mouth.

She breaths me in and nips at my tongue because she knows from previous experience that further lights my fire.

My hands move to her front and under her shirt.

I want to soak in more of her heat and feel the beat in her chest.

My knees lift to nudge, to irritate, to push her further into me and us here.

Her mouth increases pressure and I feel her suck in my mouth and tongue.

Before I can decide which way to go, she slips away and pushes her front to my back.

Now I am pinned to the tree.

"Hug the tree," she whispers in command.

As I do, she presses into me, running her hands under my shirt and up my back.

Every point of contact eliciting spark and groan.

Every soft touch pushing me.

I feel her lift up my shirt and, in a fluid motion, the skin to skin contact as her chest pushes against my back.

Her breasts slowly rotating back-and-forth, rubbing side to side across my back.

She hugs me from behind smashing those lovely mounds against my back, her hands rubbing my hip bones back to front.

I'm so aroused, I feel a delicious pain of anticipation.

Her hand slips into the front of my pants.

She finds my cock rock hard.

I feel her finger lightly brush my tip, pre-cum moistening her finger.

A forest hike has never excited me so much.

Her palm slides up and down.

Her finger brushes my tip again.

More motion up and down.

I feel boobs mashed against my back, hardened nipples scraping.

Up.

Down.

I feel her drawing me forward.

She lifts up on her toes, her hand gives my tip a gentle squeeze along the ridge.

I sense she is stopping and I'm relieved.

When I come with her today, I want satisfying finish at the end of the trail.

"More ... later," she whispers in my ear.

"When I come with you today, I want to be at our peak," she adds.

She pulls my shirt down and I turn to her.

"Agreed," I respond and watch as she offers me a mischievous grin.

Her hands trail up to her chest and she teasingly pulls on her nipples, swiping her tongue across her lips.

Then with a wink, she slowly pulls her bra and shirt back into place, gathers her pack, and heads toward the trail.

"C'mon, sweet man! Let's finish!"

Damn! I love this woman!

———

HAND IN HAND

Looking ahead, I see the end of the trail at the mountain top and the vista which is beginning to reveal itself.

He has promised a great view at the end of our eight miles.

I turn and say, "Looks like we're almost there!"

"Yes, sugar, almost."

I feel the sun on my face and the light breeze.

Trees seem to be stepping back to offer a clear view.

The warm smell of cedar on the breeze lifting my heart.

I clamber across a bit of rocky outcropping to a grassy spot and suddenly stop as the view opens drawing me in, breathless not from the hike but the beauty on display before me.

A beautiful valley makes way for dark green forest of the coastal mountain range beyond.

At the horizon I can see the gleam of blue ocean.

He comes up behind me and helps me slip off my backpack as he drops his own.

I can't look away from this spectacular vista which is just for him and me to enjoy at our leisure.

He steps up behind me, front to back.

Fully body contact.

Full body sparkle.

"Tell me what you see. Tell me what you feel," he asks.

I feel myself lean into him.

His broad shoulders anchoring me.

His hands on my waist.

His warm breath skipping across my ear.

"I see the ocean at the horizon, and it makes me think that no matter how far we go there is always more to explore, " I reply.

His hands begin a slow motion up the sides of my body.

I catch my breath as I step further into him, nestled, held.

"I see the coastal peaks and think of how they reflect the ups and downs of life," I add.

Now his hands gently cup my boobs.

I feel a tug at my core and I wiggle my butt against him, feeling his hard cock rubbing against me, his length making contact with that point where his hand is the usual visitor.

"Don't let me distract you," he whispers, while his fingers lightly rub my nipples into hard pebbles heated with new exertion.

I tune my awareness fully into the mountain man behind me.

"I feel the peak where we stand becoming our experience of this moment. I feel the sweat you have raised in me ready to drip on your hand. I feel a need which only you can fill," I whisper.

His right hand slips into the front of my hiking pants.

I hear his breathy sharp intake when he finds no panties to push aside.

His finger slides across my clit several times and then dips further down.

I take a surprised breath even though I know what he will do next.

He inserts his finger deep inside as a hook which he pulls tight inside me, bringing me up onto my toes.

"Sugar?" he breathes. "Ready?"

I exhale, "Please…"

His finger begins a come-hither motion, upside down, from my inside out, across my spongy wetness.

All the while using his hook to catch me and pull me up.

"Sugar," he breathes as his tongue swirls in my ear firing more wet up and down.

I'm losing my sense of direction, ready to ascend the peak of our joint desire.

The movement of his finger pushes and pulls, drawing out an incredible sensation of deep response.

He is so masterful, so rigid, so delicious as he melts me into him.

Into the edge of us both.

Ready to push and pull me beyond.

His finger tickles and pushes.

The motion pulling me deeper into him towards an edge as his other hand holds me around my chest as his tongue starts down the side of my neck.

I love the feeling of being taken from behind, within the open air.

Sun warming our bodies.

A soft breeze fanning the heat of our hearts.

Now his hand begins the final ascent.

He knows exactly how to trip my wire and send me flying.

A deep fingered push, an insistent full arm pull.

I groan loud enough I hear an echo paced with an incredibly hard release that sends me across the valley.

I'm gushing and his hand is drenched.

He pauses, holding me like a limp rag doll.

Hanging in his arms, he kisses my shoulder, then my neck.

More sparkle.

I see the horizon, feeling us touch the edge between my heart and his.

Mountain as firm launch pad.

Sun as halo to our coming peaks.

His hand slowly pulls out of my core.

A fingertip pushes at my lips and then slides in.

I suck his tip and run my tongue across the length of his broad long digit, tasting his sweat and my honey mixed into sweet delight.

Then I watch as he draws his hand to his mouth.

I hear him hungrily lick his fingers, knowing what he is tasting, feeling myself re-heating, preparing, knowing he is not done with either of us.

His hand sneaks under my shirt, shoving my sports bra up as my boobs drop into his warm, strong hands.

He begins to let me fall away from him as he kneads, pulls, and massages what I know he thinks of as my marshmallows.

I giggle – wanting to make s'more with him.

I open my eyes and gasp because he has me extending from the peak like I'm ready to take flight.

My feet are trapped and held by his feet while his hands have me leaning out, cantilevered from the mountaintop.

"Ready to fly, sugar?"

I shake my head yes, unable to vocalize, starting to shake, anticipating the surprise that awaits.

He pulls me in, clasping me to him front to back, top to bottom, no space between.

Every touch bringing more sparkle like bubbles rising from a geyser ready to burst.

Hands to my sides, his thumbs hook my waist band and he pulls down.

The warm breeze sends chills into all my heated places.

I tremble in anticipation.

His finger hooks itself into my pussy again.

His other hand, following the trails between my butt cheeks, hooks me from my back side.

I realize that somewhere he has dropped his pants as he lifts me to my toes, caught between fingers pulling me a part.

The hand behind becomes a hand to my boobs as he simultaneously lifts me up and slightly out.

I feel his rigid cock tuck itself in between my legs and brush my lower lips.

Moving me gently, slightly back and forth I feel his rigid head push and brush.

Liquid runs down my legs as a tiny tremor rolls through my core.

He slowly brings me back toward his chest.

In a smooth motion which feels deliberately slow, he releases his hooking finger and I slide quickly down his long shaft.

Oh! Damn! The Sparkle!

Especially as his tip hits my very sensitive inner edge.

I come, shooting light filling my awareness.

We have entered the primordial which exists within the deepest of us.

I feel him pull back, his tip rubbing my outer lips.

Heated wetness running down my thighs.

As he moves back in, he lets me fall down his rigid rod.

His girth has thickened even more, and my legs move out to allow him full entry.

The sparkle is intense taking away any awareness of time and place.

Again, he withdraws but does not leave me behind.

His fingers grip my nipples, kneading, pulling, stretching me beyond.

I feel myself tremble as another orgasm quakes me, pushing, pulling, demanding shake, my body in full shiver.

But I do not leave even though I'm ready to take off.

I await him, wanting more than anything to follow him, hand in hand, on the journey which beckons us both.

I relax, I yield, but do not submit.

Instead, I push back.

He does, too.

I scream, "Don't stop!"

He rams his luscious cock deep inside me, where my heart and soul reside.

"More! Now!" I demand, pushing him on.

He responds again, pushing at our deepest places.

Aligned, ready, knowing that the moment is primed within the divine timing that is us in this moment.

Not too fast.

Not too slow.

Instead – hard, decisive, intent.

A rod divining the focus of celestial union.

There … now!

We both let go and jump together into the exquisite experience of his sparkle and mine made only for us, by us.

In this the moment of edge – a wonderful, primal release.

A roar of delight made manifest.

He pumps me full, liquid nirvana in synch with hearts' beat.

He pulls me to him, and I come again pushed against his pulse and his heat.

He nuzzles his nose just under my ear and licks, nipping my neck.

Slowly we sink to the grass, cuddling, his arms pulling me in, his legs encasing mine.

Breath finally catching up.

Hearts connected.

Souls fully, soundly touched.

A warm, comforting sparkle surrounding, holding us safe.

My hunter.

He slays me.

I am his bounty and he, mine.

BELLY HAND

In life, simplicity is best.

I step out of the shower and gently run my linen towel across my arms and legs, catching moisture, drying skin.

Lifting one leg then the other, I softly smooth jasmine body oil across calf and thigh, down arm and around my neck, the fragrance casting pleasant memories to occupy my heart.

I reach for cotton and pull my lacy white nightgown over my head knowing the material will absorb the oil's fragrance.

Turning off lights as I go, I pad down the hall to my bedroom which is dark and cool.

A lovely night breeze gently blows the wispy white curtains.

Sitting on the edge of my bed, I kick off my slippers and silently open to the best part of my day.

I lie on my side, head on pillow and before I 've completely relaxed, a hand behind me reaches for my waist and pulls me in, insistent.

I feel delightfully claimed.

I sigh as the hand pulls once again and I roll into a sturdy, warm body.

Another hand lifts my head and hair, arranging, as one arm slips beneath my pillow and the other arm snakes across my waist, settling hand on my belly, pulling me in.

My butt feels his hard, upper thighs which bend around me, one leg lifting and intertwining with one of mine.

That hand on my belly pulls me tighter still and the upper arm tugs me in so my head rests in that sweet spot just below his chin.

We both breathe in deeply, together.

I dig into him deeper, wriggling my butt against him, pushing my shoulders into his chest.

I sigh.

At peace.

Lovingly held.

I feel his nose sniff along my neck.

I shift just a bit to let him go the full length, from ear to shoulder.

I feel the wet warmth of his tongue caress a sore spot.

The belly hand finds the top of my spine and begins to massage a line down my back.

A tingly shiver follows his fingertips and when he is done, he pulls me back in, hand to belly.

Another joint deep breath and we settle into the bed, cocooned in warmth, the feather comforter pulled up to my nose.

He and I have done wild, wonderful crazy things together, in bed and out.

But this, this alignment of bodies for sleep, is intimate simplicity at its best.

To feel taken in, claimed, nurtured, loved, completely touched by simply being held is for me the most profound feeling.

More than cuddling or spooning because he offers not only his body, but in the settling in I feel enveloped by his heart and soul.

I open and return the depths of my being to him.

The extraordinary peace which fills us both hits the very core of me and him.

I touch him on all levels and he, me.

As I fall into sleep, I feel tears slip down my face and his fingertips trace their flow, gently wiping them away.

He whispers in my ear, "Baby, I'm here. I've got you!"

And, once again, belly hand pulls me in.

MY SUGAR NOW

LEANING INTO UNCERTAINTY

THE PADS OF HIS FINGERS SLIDE SLOWLY, SOFTLY DOWN THE left side of my face.

Heat flowing in the movement, turning my cold skin warm for a moment until the now revealed skin is touched by the edge of the cold November morning.

Though, I know the chill will be brief because anticipation of his hand's return raises its own heat.

Plus, we have an agreement about his fingers on my face.

I am leaning against the railing which surrounds a 20-foot deck cantilevered into a stand of huge redwood trees.

Looking above, the magnificent trees reach like a cathedral into a cloudy sky.

The tops in morning fog, little fingers reaching down with a slow brush of autumn air.

Fog limiting the view to just the outside edges of the deck.

Behind me, he stands as sentinel, holding me in place with the stillness of his mountain demeanor.

I come alive in the pressure of his body against mine and the clear awareness of his solid presence.

He is not aggressive, rather assertive.

Not angry, determined.

Not passive, always with clearly focused intention.

He is the mountain man I have waited for.

When he first showed in my life, I thought he might be a man of few words.

I was hesitant because I want the parley of relationship where words trill first like a flute, then descend into the heated vibration of bass, and finally settle into multi-symphonic exchange.

Hearts weaving together within the sharing of both the silent and the verbal, the expressive and the physical.

The words of other men have been deceptive and, on further knowing, fell flat in superficial shine.

Not with him.

No, I have found instead he is a man of worded intention, clear in his communication, fully present to himself and to me.

Clearly competent.

Not perfect, but rather able to deal and attend to the detail of the moment and the expansive arc of the full journey.

He didn't take long to show me what he wanted with me, from me.

His words followed by adoring action, his clarity opening a door between us, which supports me in my own clarity and my own desire.

He offered and I willingly received, held in a heated circle of yearning born from the intersection of us two, body, mind, heart, and soul.

With other men, I have always felt a separation, a false boundary between various aspects of our lives.

Now we eat, now we walk, now we have sex.

But, with him, each moment is a communion born of our integration which began in the simplicity of question and response, offering and receiving.

A willingness to learn the other.

A desire to release walls and see the other in the beauty of the moment.

Tracing the nuance of shift and the emergence of newness born from all levels of exchange.

For me a mountain man is a wild man, freed from the restraints of personal history, choosing to step beyond into the edges of the unknown.

HE KNOWS THAT THE BEST, THE DEEPEST PART OF relationship arises in this willingness to invite uncertainty.

THE SAVOR BEGINS

I remember the moment on our third date when this aspect emerged fully in my vision of him.

He had arranged a hike to one of my favorite locations: a butte rising from the edges of the Columbia River.

We climb to the top, spread a beautiful red blanket, and sit down together, circled by large blue skies and a panoramic horizon with views of high plateau, Mount Adams to the north, Mount Hood to the south, and a deep, wide river flowing at the base of the butte below us.

He surprises me with my favorite picnic of grilled flat iron steak topped with chimichurri sauce and a fruity yet deep Malbec to drink.

He has even carried in stemless wine glasses.

We begin our picnic about 4 PM on an August day.

The weather is warm just to the edge of hot and the soft breeze creates an easy cooling retreat from the hurries of the world.

The biggest surprise: he has clearly remembered my responses on our first date about favorite locations and foods.

As we sit there soaking in the natural presence and our connection with and between, he asks this question:

"What's most important to you in exploring the sexual level of a relationship?"

By this point, I have learned of his ability to ask directly and his desire to learn me.

We have already tasted each other.

I know the feel of his lips and the heat of his tongue.

I know the comfort and the challenge of his body pressed firmly against mine.

I know from our hugs, I invite his deepest, hardest responses as the press of his rigid cock brings out the wetness of my desire for him.

A desire which began as a circling into each other.

A spiral drawing us into a sacred space we hold for each other.

Our first meeting was the standard meet and greet.

Thirty minutes in I knew I wanted see him again.

I stood up.

Put on my coat and took a piece of paper from my pocket.

I was going old school.

I place the paper on the table.

"Thank you for meeting me. I'd enjoy seeing you again. Here's my phone number if you want to see me as well."

I smiled, turned around, and headed toward the door.

At the door, I turn to see him watching me.

I smile and wave hoping this won't be the last view of this amazing man.

Two days later, he calls and asks me out.

On our first date, we agreed that the best relationship comes in the willingness to learn and to share, openly and honestly.

"You're not someone I want to fuck and move on from," he explained at the end of that first exchange.

"No, I want to learn you, please. I don't want to hurry. You deserve to be savored, one breath at a time."

He had said this with a look which was both intensely certain and plainly hopeful.

His brown eyes shining with anticipation, the motion of his eyebrows expressing his wish that I return a response agreeing that my desire aligned with his.

I heard his words with a jump of anticipation and a heated coil rising within me.

I had never felt this so strongly.

The coil begins a purr and a fiery vibrational response.

All of him – his words, his presence, his inner simmer combined with his wide hands, strong shoulders, and a sharp-edged face kindled my desire to know all of him.

I told him that savor was a great word, both active response and hopeful description of a new beginning.

"Yes, sweet man, my hope is that we are more a multi-course meal than five minutes of fast food."

Sitting on the butte, his question came within this expanding context of a relationship built on exploration and a willingness to learn the other.

That's how I answered him.

"For me continual exploration is key. So is intention and honesty and agreement and communication. I want a continual process of learning so that we can respond without hesitation or limitation, beyond the stagnant surface."

"Mmmm…I like that a lot," he responds.

We both pause.

His eyes are fixed on mine, a warm smile focused on me.

I believe he likes what he sees in me.

His words for me often include beautiful and sexy.

This has helped me past some of my insecurity that my curves are not lovable and that my less than supermodel height is a bother for this tall man.

When we hug, my head fits perfectly just under his chin, his arms pull me in and I nestle in this warmth feeling safe and adored.

"And you? What's most important for you?" I ask, offering him a sip of wine.

He sips and sets the glass down.

He smiles at me and reaches out to retrieve a piece of steak.

Then leans towards me bringing the meat to my mouth, holding it so that I can take a bite of the longish piece.

I bite and chew and take a sip of wine, relishing the mingled tastes and the sunny breeze on my face.

In his smile, I let go of our surroundings and my eyes are for him only.

In return he is watching me, enjoying himself and me.

I lean toward him looking at the remaining steak in his hand.

He brings his fingers towards my mouth.

I take hold of his wrist and bring his hand the rest of the way.

My tongue reaches out and I gently lick his fingers and then suck his fingers and the steak into my mouth, allowing my tongue to caress his fingers and relieve him of his offered treasure.

He leans in and kisses me, pouring wine into my mouth through his lips.

I feel the edges of him and the edges of me melting, blending together in the flow.

Arising vibration of both excitement and contentment.

Knowing I am exactly where I want to be.

"I believe the exploration we both want has begun very well," he answers.

"For me I want to know your limits and your desires, and I want you to know mine. Because I want our relationship to explore our edges always. How does that sound to you?"

Before answering, I turn my head away from him and absorb more sun and the incredible view of Mt. Hood rising in the distance.

Even turned away, I feel him absorbing me.

I return my gaze to him and respond.

"I think I understand but let's be clear. What do you mean about edges?"

"Good question. You're asking me to define terms."

He stretches out on our blanket turning toward me, his head balanced on his hand.

"Yes," I respond.

"I don't want to assume or take you for granted and would ask the same from you, " he offers.

"Agreed," I respond.

His hand reaches out and gently rubs my bare shin.

A shiver blooms upward.

He continues, "Edges, for me, are opportunities to learn, to explore, to know each other. To venture together beyond into the unknown. I'm not content repeating the same old. I want to see how far I can push myself on all levels. And I'd like a partner who feels the same."

His finger continues the shiver dance on my other shin.

He can't touch me that I don't respond instinctively.

Takes little for him to get my sizzle in motion.

"In a relationship, are edges only with sex?" I ask.

"Oh, no. Not at all. Edges are everywhere — that's what makes relationship so exciting and challenging and confusing."

He laughs and raises another piece of steak for me and gently shoves his fingers into my mouth.

My tongue caresses and I suck the bite away from his grasp.

"Mmmmm....yummy!" I exclaim.

The taste of him mixing with the greenness of the chimichurri is wonderful.

Edges always it seems with him and me.

In the short time of our acquaintance, we have both challenged and met the other at the intersection of our unknowns.

His eyes shine with amusement.

"However, the edges of sex are delicious when jointly shared, don't you think?"

Any idea that this guy can't or won't communicate are completely obliterated.

His fingers now running up and down my leg, combined with his words and his grin, blow me open.

He might as well be sucking on my clit because all this now has a similar effect on me.

I love the sharing of minds as prelude to the deeper dance.

I cross my ankles trapping his hand, slowing the buzz so I can speak.

But he squeezes my leg and continues speaking before I can respond.

"One of the things I noticed early on about you. You're both playful and serious. Able to leap from one to the other like a playful kitten leaping into the air and landing as an owl full of wisdom."

His smile becomes even more heated.

His fingers grip my leg, his thumb mindlessly tracing a trail.

I stop.

My breath hitching, fluttering at his words as the heat of desire makes a leap within me.

I shift as his offered observation uncovers me.

I am seen.

I feel the intoxicating energy exuded by this man seeping deeper, further into me, and stealing another breath.

He raises wonder in me, and I want to know more at the same time I want to lean into him and explode, losing awareness yet gaining that elusive perception which comes when one plus one equals infinity.

A blush rises across my face and down my back and front.

Then it happens for the first time.

He reaches towards me.

His finger pads lightly stroke the heat of my blush from cheek down the side of my face.

I feel more heat churn, drawing me to him.

His light touch again on my face, a slow ignite that has a depth which cannot come from a quick strike.

I lean into the edge created by his smooth slide and I feel a yearning bloom within me, pushing me to step into his edge.

I plunge.

There is no going back.

That I will be beyond, a different person with him, because of him – it's my yearning.

Not me giving up me.

No, instead both of us as we each are, learning to be more.

I'm getting exactly what I've always wanted.

And though there is that slight ripple of *Am I good enough?*

With him, the promise of exploration moves us into a different arena where vulnerability is a launchpad into expansion and not an indictment of me as unequal to the experience of shared growth and sexual adventure.

"I want to know your edges," I begin, feeling a smaller flush on my face.

It's not been easy for me to learn that I am safe with him in my own clarity.

"My sense of you is that you know edges I do not yet know but yearn to experience."

I kiss the end of my pinky finger and lay it gently on his lips.

"Please?" I ask.

He sucks in my pinky, swirling his tongue around the tip, lightly sucking.

He draws back letting my finger lightly rest on his lips.

"That I can do, sugar," he whispers, pulling me down with him, on to the blanket and into a deep full body embrace.

————

HEAT SIGNALS

From that moment to now, we have continued the conversation begun on the butte.

We have learned much about each other.

In a sense, he is kinkier than me.

But that's more a description of his history compared to mine — may be better to say he has had more opportunity than me to explore beyond vanilla.

For a bit he was a Dom which he says helped him focus the intent of his desire, to bring forward his wild, and direct his pursuit of edge.

In the experience he stepped beyond the dazzle and the superficial to find that most dungeons hid the depth he learned he most desired.

For him control is not the goal, but rather a process to move beyond the everyday into the experience beyond.

Though different in experience, I have the same desire for depth beyond the feeling that the only possibility in relationship is to settle for the same old in a limited fifteen minutes once a week.

We have agreed that what we both want is a constant exchange which emerges from the daily joy of learning each other.

To this end, we have several agreements which cover what each wants, what each will do, and the current borders of our desires.

We even have an agreement to re-visit all this on a regular basis to refine and expand.

He loves to surprise me, and I love surprises.

He loves anticipation and so do I.

We have created a shorthand, a set of physical signals which both ask and warn, both heat and delay.

Most importantly we have granted each other free use.

Anytime, anywhere, just ask.

His surprises always take me beyond.

Partly because I know that he has been delighting himself within imagination and anticipation.

Plus, he knows that the unpredictable sets up the heat of anticipation for me.

This agreement freely made means that we bring depth everywhere we go and why I don't feel the disconcerting motion of disconnected moments with him.

Between he and I there is a continuous flow which carries us high and deep, twisting together through the threshold of the unknown.

We are both certain of who we are, and our joining is not a dissolving as much as it is a unifying of him and me in the infinite possibility of us.

His finger pads lightly stroking my face is his signal: Sugar, I want you. Now.

He knows the signal alone is sometimes enough to make me come.

A switch to raise my heat.

The click of anticipation brings the focus to him, to me, to us.

SUGAR, WHAT DO YOU WANT?

Here we stand on the redwood deck – a place which has become ours in our very early morning walks.

His finger traces my face and he leans into me, his chin resting lightly on the top of my head.

We are still standing back to front.

His other hand slips under my hooded black sweatshirt.

I hear him sucking in his breath in surprise as he realizes I left my bra at home.

I suck in my breath as his chilled fingers run up my spine.

My nipples harden and I let myself relax into him, even though everything in my body is now filled with delicious tension.

His hand now moves up the side of my body to gently cup my breast, pulling me in tighter to his body.

Leaving my face, his other hand unzips his coat and pulls me inside so that his coat envelops me with him.

His other finger tweaks my nipple.

Heat builds and another blush colors my face.

I move my hip gently against him and I can feel his cock pushed against me, caressing the valley of my ass.

More tweaking of my nipple pulls me into him and begins to stoke my internal flame.

I know that it's not likely anyone will be visiting the deck given the early hour.

But it is a public space and I know the possible exposure excites him.

This was really difficult for me at first, but I learned that most of my resistance was about trust.

He has shown me in important ways that by visiting this edge, I am learning trust in a new way.

And I have.

Or at least I know this: I trust him completely.

We stand back to front as if we are one.

The pressure of his body readies me.

I feel my core heating and liquefying.

I feel anticipation coursing through my body in waves.

Now his hand reaches into the front of my pants.

I hear him chuckle in my ear.

He has found that my bra wasn't the only piece left behind.

In my ear he whispers, "I want you now."

His finger sinks into my pussy like a hook and he pulls, lifting me to my toes.

His tongue dips into my ear.

My knees weaken a bit and I feel deliciously caught.

In a throaty whisper he asks, "Sugar, what do you want?"

Now my signal.

I push my butt into his hardness and his finger pulls on me tighter, unleashing a wetness which I can feel flow on to my inner thighs.

"You," I reply. "In two." Meaning his cock in me once, a bit shallow.

But, by two, fully hilted in what he knows will be wet, hot, and tight just for him.

"How?" He growls, rubbing into me.

"Wolf's choice," I reply.

This means not only is it his choice, but he doesn't need to tell me his plans.

More importantly for us both, I want him at his wild edge, rough and unhinged.

In other words: come on, Mr. Mountain Man, surprise me – pound me with your best!

He growls and dips his head to my neck.

Tongue lapping my neck from my shoulder up slowly to behind my ear.

Lips gliding down until teeth nip firmly at the soft skin just a bit lower than my ear.

He does this intentionally because he knows how hot it is for me to have him come from behind and how erotic and sensitive my neck is for both him and me.

But I jump a bit in surprise for now both of his hands are under my sweatshirt, twirling and pulling on my nipples.

The pull and bite create delicious sensations that are painfully pleasurable.

I wriggle, moaning, pushing against him.

He knows how much I love the assertive feel of his nip and pull.

The motion centers my awareness on him, on me, on the joining of us.

He continues to rub and pull.

His teeth move to the base of my neck, to the highly sensitive skin on my shoulders.

Our anticipation building, stoking our fires.

He pushes into my back, lifting a bit on his toes so that his hard shaft slides intently up and down between my butt cheeks.

Pulling nipples, nipping skin, pushing shaft.

He knows he has me and he continues to beckon, driving me forward.

All of my awareness is focused on him.

My body is tight in anticipation, focused on every sensation rippling in response to his touch and his pull.

"Sugar – baby mine. Now."

More a growl than a voice but definitely a clear demand.

Both of us twixt and between.

Losing the ability for coherent speech.

The furnace in me is stoked beyond and I feel first a light release, followed by the roar of fiery explosion.

"Aaaahhhh!" I yell completely focused on the ripples within me.

A crescendo, a release.

A crescendo, a release.

Lost in the feel of him.

My entire body ripples as the final wave crests and hits my shore.

I hear his chuckle and he lets my body begin to fall forward with a quick warning.

"Sugar, hold on!"

I grab the railing as he pulls down my pants.

His finger finds my slit from behind and sinks in.

Like a finger dipped in a honey pot, gathering nectar through a full swirl around the edge.

He pulls his finger out, hooking honey in the bend of his finger.

"Here, Sugar, for you."

He brings his finger to my lips.

I gently lick his fingertip, then eagerly suck his finger in entirely, loving the mix of his sweat with my juice.

Then I feel him use his foot to push my feet further apart.

He likes me wide open and a little off-balance.

I like the surrender involved.

He does not invade – he envelops me wholly and entirely.

His hand gently pushes my head down and he caresses my butt no longer bothered by the chilly weather.

I wonder what he is planning.

Past experience tells me he has a plan.

The thought of his gathering desire pulls out more shivered anticipation in me.

Whack! His first slap on my butt stings.

I feel a heated compression chase the chilly air.

The second slap, on the other side, catches my breath and excites me beyond reason.

I now know the path he has chosen for this moment.

The prospect of this journey makes me even wetter and definitely tighter.

Before him, I never knew this delicious edge which somehow transforms my fear into joy, my doubt into ecstasy.

He has this way of flicking his hands at just the right angle where the slap ignites more heat and pushes me further into what I can take and transform into pleasure.

In between each rasp, he slowly licks the point of contact.

Every beat in a slightly different timing and at a slightly different location.

Keeping me guessing, keeping in me in an extraordinary tension which disconnects me again from nothing but the awareness of his hand and the syncopation of his hallowed beats.

The sting of the slap combined with the evaporation of each lick creates a delicious competition of sensation across the plane of my body.

I know I will be red and sore, but his attention to my body pulls me to a suspended space of exquisite pleasure.

I lose count and lose myself in his hand.

My heated pulse beating in double time with each slap.

Now his finger finds my clit.

I'm so wet that he need not find lubrication.

His finger lightly taps my nub, repeating the random beat of his slaps.

Each tap more insistent than the previous.

Tap. Tap. Tap.

I have moved to a space of complete release.

He can do anything.

I willingly follow.

His teeth nibble again at my neck.

His tongue grazes my ear.

He whispers, "Ready, Sugar? Baby mine."

He begins anew on my clit.

Tap. Tap. Tap.

I have focus only for his taps.

Light as they may be, they are insistent.

He is gentle, but clearly telling me what he believes I have within me to repeat.

Like a trainer insisting on the extra reps.

Tap. Tap. Tap.

From our time on the butte, he has been helping me explore the edges of sensation and experience, introducing new ways for me to learn a deeper experience, a further path.

Somewhere in the mist of our worship, I feel the last remainder of resistance within me fade.

It's not strong enough any longer.

It's lost its fight.

I am profoundly touched as I feel his taps pull it out of me, clearing my shore, making my only choice to follow his insistent finger.

Tap. Tap. Tap.

Another inner burden lets go.

Bringing me all of sudden face to face with a damn I have always felt within me.

A damn I never thought I could break.

A damn which seemed to block me from a deeper road.

Tap. Tap. Tap.

The damn cracks.

Everything within me breaks forward and up and through and down and away and returns to cycle again through the electric power of his finger on my clit.

Tap. Tap. Tap.

In the breath of the damn crash comes a tidal wave which shakes me to the depths of my soul, toes to head, fingertip to fingertip.

I can't tell if I stand or if I fall or if I float.

But in the release, I shake full body and he delivers another slap that powers another body quake.

I freefall peak to valley, losing the limits of self.

Tender hands hold me.

Tender whispers center me.

Tenderness caresses me.

I am present without concern, with trust, with him.

There is no stopping, only a pushing forward.

His cock pushes into my core.

Slowly, almost too slow.

Surprised because usually by this point, I am done.

Today is different.

Old barriers now gone.

Instead, I feel a new me cleared of the old.

I am focused, ready, wanting to ride with him to his shore.

He comes to a stop and bends over me whispering in my ear, "Sugar, you're mine."

Then he slowly, slowly pulls out and I know he knows anticipation is tripping me into the stars.

He can feel the tiny sparks blooming as I feel myself begin to embrace the promise of another high tide.

I feel us hanging in the stillness were all becomes an experience beyond time.

Our edges are fraying and melting together, moving us beyond.

Now his hand comes to the back of my neck, and he pulls my hair into his hand.

I push back at him trying to hurry him.

He chuckles, "Not yet, Sugar."

His desire coalescing into a joining.

His lead transforming us both into more.

He gently pulls my head up with his hand in my hair and he whispers, "Now."

He slams his length into me, and time slows.

Like we both have suddenly gotten longer and deeper, his motion and mine stretch time so that our shared explosion lasts forever and creates a multi-color flare felt in every cell and in every synapse of desire.

A chain of give and receive in an endless feedback loop freely exchanged.

I scream as another wave hits me.

I hear his groan ebb from his depths.

I push into him trying to melt us together in our shared heat.

I feel his heart stutter and then thunder.

His hand pulls me up, so we are fully body to body, his hands on my breasts holding me up.

His cock still firmly within me.

The motion sets him off again and he crushes me in his arms and his lips as he buries his steel shaft in me with a determination born of wild desire.

Finding my neck, he nips, and his throaty growl lets me know he is satisfied with his wolfish choice.

Our hearts are beating hard.

I feel him, breath not yet stilled, body taunt keeping us both up.

I swear he has just catapulted us into the canopy of the watching trees.

We fly, suspended in the timeless connection of our mutual desire.

As we land, I am supported by the peak of this man and the delicious mountain of our now ebbing flame.

I feel sweat soaking into my sweatshirt and a cold wind blowing across my bare legs.

His heated breath in my ear and down my neck.

He slips out and inserts a finger into the depth of me.

Wriggling his fingertip as deep as he can go.

Then he pulls out.

Then I hear lips smacking.

He leans into me and lightly pulls his finger down the side of my face.

His lips right at my ear, he whispers, "Yes, baby mine. You are my sugar. The hot, awesome bubbly kind!"

I pull up my pants and lean into him, gazing at the forest beyond our deck, noticing that there is now more to see though fog and mist are still part of the view.

I smile and offer my own claim, "Come on, sweet man. You are my sugar, too."

His fingertips continue to lightly caress the side of my face, warming me.

His tongue lightly traces my ear and he chuckles, "Sugar, I'll race you home."

I turn to see the grin on his face and the happy twinkle in his eyes.

I push my fingers into his upper arm.

"Tag! You're it!" I yell and take off running down the path, laughing so hard I trip.

Right behind, he catches me and pulls me into a tight bear hug.

He whispers, "Sugar just know sometime before we get home, I will signal. OK?"

Damn! I love this man!

"OK!" I respond. "But only if you can catch me!"

We take off down the trail, both of us knowing he can catch me at any time.

Sweet anticipation, building sugar, heating not just from the running but from our edges melting.

Both us ready for the signal:

My Sugar ... now.

AGAINST THE WALL

Pressed against the ancient stone, my breasts buried in the moss, nipples rubbing against solid roughness brings instant heat.

The cool autumn breeze washes against my bare butt with a chill which oddly stokes my heat.

His breath in my ear focuses me clearly on us, here, now.

"Lift your arms, baby," he growls.

I rest my arms across the stone above me, feeling deliciously caught between two planes of hardness.

One chilled from the autumn weather.

The other heated from exertion and building excitement.

His finger probes between wall and me, searching for my opening.

We are at the base of an old bridge and he, who has free use, has firmly caged me against the stone embankment.

The air is filled with mist and tendrils of fog.

We have already hiked six miles and we both have skin steeped with heat and steam and sweat.

"I want your heat, baby," he growls and licks my ear as his finger slips into my opening.

"Ohhh!" I groan as he hooks and pulls.

I squeeze his fingers, trapping, gaining more force, more awareness of his motion in and out.

"Baby ..." he growls. "You're always so ready," he whispers.

I smile knowing he knows that I know that it is our play, our agreements, and our willingness to visit our edges which fuels our fire.

I begin to reply and stop my words but not the heat that is building.

Footsteps sound on the bridge above us. Laughter. People talking.

My pulse picks up.

Is discovery happening?

I clench my mouth tight, close my eyes, and bear down on his fingers, willing myself not to make a sound.

Neither of us with the intention to stop, to take cover.

Yet, I know that the possibility of being seen will push him on.

He won't stop because he loves the dare and the excitement.

And I'm not wrong.

His cock slams into me, pushing me up the wall a bit, dragging my boobs on the roughness.

A pleasurable pain all around.

I clench in the groan willing it to fade within me.

Letting his motion be our only shared sound.

He has always completely filled me.

While he is mostly buried in me now, he is not all the way.

I can take more.

However, he is taking his time, hoping, that every thrust will make me lose myself and utter the noise which will attract attention.

He likes to be discovered.

He likes to watch my blush rise up my face and down my butt.

Initially, I was embarrassed to feel exposed, to allow a public eye on what I wanted to be a private act.

Whether because he sensed my unease or because he did this instinctively, after the first stroke or two, he covers me with his body – part of the reason for my hands above my head.

Though he takes his time, we will finish while he protects me from prying eyes.

Now, I'm willing to go against the wall wherever he asks.

With my eyes closed and utterly focused, anywhere is just him and me.

Now, his weight as he thrusts into me takes me beyond.

I lose time and space.

Just him.

Me.

The wall.

My wet, hot core.

His rigid shaft.

Most importantly, safe space.

He has shown me how to trust.

How to yield.

How to let go and come undone.

Against the wall, he has me, knows me, holds me.

Whether a minute or an hour, I am only present to his motion, his willingness to take me up and out and in.

I feel his chest against my back, and I feel his cock hit against my depth.

His chest pinning me, as he draws back.

His fingers intertwining with mine.

I can feel all his length, firm thighs to bulky arms – his entire body pressed against me.

I feel the roil of our heat building.

I feel my core liquefying and dripping into him.

He and me.

No words, yet he speaks with his body slamming against mine.

I want all of him against me, in me.

My knees begin to loosen as my core tightens.

Between one breath and the next, he takes me up and I fall into bliss, a ruptured heat, boiling.

The roughness of the wall pushing me, the roughness of his motion softening my resistance.

Until … leaving people and stone behind … just him and me.

I let go.

He, too, goes hard.

We soar into the beat of his body and mine.

Sharing explosive flight.

Ragged edges softened with heat.

Two bodies pressing ancient stone.

For he takes me … always … against the wall.

FINGER DRAG

HE PHONED AND SAID COME HOME AND I DID. I LEFT SEVERAL errands undone because I could hear the urgent heat in his voice. I didn't speed, but I drove the coast road with a focused intent. Home, now.

Turning from the highway to follow the gravel road to our place. A small two-bedroom cottage set about 1000 yards from the Pacific Ocean. Only three other houses sharing our road. Each home separated and enclosed by a grand forest of large alder, huge fir, and several guardian cedars.

We both work from home with flexible schedules which gives us the space to entertain each other both on a whim and on somewhat of a schedule.

His request today is not scheduled. His request might be unexpected, but I am fully aware of his intention, his desire.

Reaching out as he did when he knew my mind was probably elsewhere, he was quickly and effectively diverting my attention to him, to us.

As I pull into the short driveway, I see him standing at the front door.

He smiles and points to the end of the house.

I understand this signal having received it many times before.

He wants me to let him unload the car while I enter the house from the back deck.

I nod, turn off the car, and make my way around the end of the building.

Ahead of me is the view which always takes my breath. A wide flat beach and the rolling waves of the Pacific Ocean. The best the Oregon Coast has to offer.

Today the wind is cool, sharp, and moist, invigorating like most Autumn days are here seemingly at the end of the world. In the foreground, the horizon melds with the endless ocean. Behind me the forest is endless, a support system for our lives, a connection with all that is.

There's a strength in the view and in the nature which surrounds me in this place, filling me with quiet, strength, and peaceful comfort.

Whatever might not be enough, inside our home he fills us with the same strength and purpose as the ocean and the wind.

I enter the French doors of our bedroom leaving the door open a bit to hear the surf and fill me and the room with the salty ocean air.

Immediately I see the purpose of his call.

On the wall – our wall – a large index card with the thick, bold strokes of one single word: HERE.

My heart jumps with excitement as I feel myself relax because I understand the sign.

HERE is where he is headed and where he intends to find me.

For this sign, he has two favorite locations.

The first is the wall just outside the door I just entered. Painted charcoal gray, he loves the contrast between my flesh and the outdoor space. He also loves the exposure and the pushing roar of the ocean especially on cloudy days inflaming us both with the challenge of the elements.

The second is the red wall opposite our bed where I stand now. Here he adores how his touch creates blushes across my body which match the background color. He enjoys the play of the coziness of our private space connected through the infinity of glassed walls and doors with the forest and ocean beyond.

Because the sign is on this red wall, I understand what he is asking me to do.

I feel a joy in my heart because I know he has been thinking and considering and contemplating me and him and the possibilities of our time together.

That it is the red wall bodes well for me, though the outdoor wall is also always in my favor.

That it is the red wall means that I only need do one thing: take off my shoes and my coat, and stand with my back facing the wall, eyes closed.

I do this and take a deep breath.

The breath brings in the salty air and the quiet of our home.

Because all the sounds are from outside, I do not hear him.

But still I stand, keeping myself in the moment, using the roar from outside to quiet my mind even though my body is beginning to warm in anticipation.

I feel a shift from within and the quiet motion of body moving quietly, intently through our space.

He doesn't make a sound, but the intimate closeness of our connection helps me feel his motion wherever he is and especially when he is making his way toward me.

Eyes closed, I await his approach.

I await his touch.

I feel him enter the room and turn my head in his direction, eyes still closed.

The drag of his finger down my arm creates a fierce, fiery chill across my skin.

A flow of warmth radiating as his finger slowly, intently traces a path along the outside of my bare arm.

I can feel my knees wanting to buckle, but the intensity of the drag is enough levitation to keep me upright.

I feel the smooth wall behind me also giving support to push into his touch, into his fingers pulling on my skin.

My focused desire is to stay in touch, fully connected.

Another drag of his warm fingers on my other arm and we have begun.

His thumb tracing the edge of my jaw and chin.

A finger dragging across this temple and then the other.

I lose track of time and have no idea how long I have been suspended between his fingers and the wall.

But I don't need time.

All I need is awareness of the moment with him and the luscious drag of his finger.

Every drag pushes me against the wall.

I let time go.

I let him lead.

Fingers now dragging down the sides of both arms. A feathery touch which fires my skin.

Heat conducting between my skin and his finger drag.

Every motion, whether thumb or forefinger, pushes my attention away from the clock and fixes awareness at exactly one point.

A singular focus where his finger touches my skin – where his desire intersects with my need.

My awareness flicks across our beginnings when the opportunity for drag began.

Maybe I should have been a bit more withdrawn initially.

Perhaps a bit coy or a little standoffish.

However, I've never succeeded at playing games with anyone, particularly men.

I am very much WYSIWYG – what you seek is what you gain.

I accept the deal as dealt, willing to show my cards, willing to quickly move past the shallow and the superficial.

A dive into deep waters is me.

My surprise with him?

Before I could express my perspective, he left the shore and swam past me into the deep.

Then beckoned my approach, my vulnerability, my acceptance of him and his depth.

A challenge we both adore.

A challenge we both need to share with the other.

Now his finger entices, inviting me to join where breath is jointly inhaled, and the dive becomes collaborative endeavor.

He offers and I accept.

We sail past superficial, past game, past pretense.

Now we dive – always together.

His finger on my skin a preamble, an invitation, a challenge.

How much can I take?

How much can I receive?

How long can I last?

How long will he delay?

In the early days, he quietly gathered awareness of me, about me.

He took time to know me.

He asked about my desires and my wants and my won'ts.

We shared specifics and we each made a list to exchange of desired surprise and private fantasy.

He questioned me and I him.

One day I told him I thrive on touch.

Yet, for most of my life I have been starved of the pleasure of this shared connection.

Hands held on beach walks, the cuddle on the couch, the snuggle after sex, the embrace as we both slip into sleep.

Like an explorer in the wilderness, he learned me and catalogued my desire.

He learned also that I will follow his lead because I have learned that this stokes the depths of his yearning and gives him what he has always wanted and never received.

My willingness to exchange depth in the banter, to let his fire build through the teasing he directs at me.

He is not a man who desires fast, cheap food.

He is more interested in many courses with a girl who reads, a woman wickedly capable with the philosophical and the spiritual.

He wants a lover who is good, giving, and game for the intellectual as well as the sensual.

Shared adventure on the road less travelled, learning together, moment to moment.

Now he puts his learning of me into action.

Using what his has gathered, he flirts with me.

Sometimes it is just words, a comment, a conversation about whatever is on his mind.

Sometimes words are not needed and he finds powerful expression with finger and arm, lips and legs.

Never an empty tease.

Rather as ritual, as the opening to joint share.

He fills my tanks, pushing me to overfill and drown in the flirt – taking in more than I ever imagined I could receive.

The ritual of delicious touch begins with a smile which becomes extraordinarily heated as he lets me know that I have no choice.

Today the smile began on the phone.

In his motion around me, even though my eyes are stilled closed, I feel his smile and his enjoyment of me and mine.

The time has come for him to take the next step, to open our deep path.

He edges towards me, guiding with slow steps as he maneuvers me firmly against our red wall.

I trust his guidance.

I am ready for whatever he has in mind.

I feel his breath heat and catch.

Connected with the wall, his finger presses against the base of my neck and drags downward stopping just before the little valley and the swell of my breasts.

My breath catches as well.

Heat blossoms in the touch, jumping like electric charges at every point of contact.

At the delta of our touch, we breath together. A depth of anticipation.

He is never in a hurry – always focused on my response

The the longer he draws me out, the longer he has me at his mercy, and the more powerful will be our journey.

He lifts his finger to my mouth.

I softly kiss the instrument he will use to inflame my desire.

A brief flicker within me and I wonder how I look to him: confident in anticipation, uncertain about accepting, or caught in extreme need? Maybe a little of all three?

Either way, he never hesitates.

He brings his finger to his mouth and lightly blows on the spot wet from my mouth.

I feel the whispered blow directed at me.

Not restraining myself, a whimper comes from me as I finally open my eyes.

Dressed only in his baggy gray sweatpants, I know where he is headed. I feel a wetness gathering in my core.

A response to his drag and that this incredible man is entirely focused on me.

"Arm up," he whispers.

I lift my left arm, hand now at shoulder height, quivering in anticipation.

He gently touches my shoulder joint with just one finger.

His finger slowly traces the top of my bare arm from shoulder to elbow.

Now he presses gently into the inside crevice of my elbow and traces a circle.

So slow is his finger drag, I feel every feather graze ignite each synapse, each tiny point of connection between my skin and his finger.

I can't help my response and I don't try.

Another shiver runs through me.

His fingers always invite a full and complete response.

But a response which is more like reaction because I don't plan anything.

I simply let whatever he raises in me to fully express.

To just be as he invites to me be and feel.

Again, I whimper and trace my lips with my tongue.

His finger continues the journey now from elbow to wrist.

His leg moves slightly between my legs, pinning me to the wall.

From prior experience he knows to make sure I stay upright and in touch with the drag.

Now his finger flows onto my palm and down the length of my middle finger.

Pulling back, he kisses his fingertip and then presses the fingered kiss into my hand.

I feel his moisture on my heated skin.

Leaning forward, he whispers into my ear, "Arm up."

Without thought, my right arm raises.

His finger begins the same journey.

First shoulder to elbow.

Now a tender circle at the crevice.

Then elbow to palm and a gentle yet heated finger kiss.

The light touch is exquisite and slightly tickles.

I feel a shiver shake my body and I wiggle against him.

"Babe," he growls, "Stand still."

I close my eyes and feel myself sinking into the feel of his finger on my arm, on my palm, on my finger.

The ritual continues and he repeats.

First one side then the other.

New trails, first across the bottom of both arms, then across the tops.

A gentle light touch which sparks me again and again.

Each motion fulfillment.

Each drag a gift to me satiating the bottomless tank of my desire that only he has taken the time to figure out how to nourish and sustain.

Now he signals a change.

The tip of his tongue lightly traces my ear.

Wetness begins – no continues, stronger, deeper.

His fingers hook the hem of my tank top and in a swooshing breeze, he pulls the tank off and drops it on the floor.

His fingers go to both of my hands.

In unison, each drag along my arms, stopping to lightly caress the tender skin at my elbows.

Then his fingertips lightly drag on the skin below my clavicles until one thumb lightly caresses a nipple poking through the lacy material of my bra.

I shake even though I know his direction and his destination.

He leans toward me a bit more and whispers in my ear. "Sugar, you're incredibly hot."

I begin to reply but am halted by his motion.

Finger joins thumb, he pulls and twists each nipple as his tongue lands in the nook just behind my ear lobe.

His mouth hardens my body.

His knee at my core adds encouragement to push into him.

"Babe," he whispers.

A solitary finger drags across my arms.

His fingers intertwine with mine.

His entire body pushes into mine.

His tongue trails across my lips.

The hardness of his cock rubbing , pushing me to keep standing.

As I try to lift my lips to his, he pulls back and reminds me, "Babe, I give, you receive."

He lifts my hands above my head.

Pulling me up slightly, he slowly rotates my body.

My back to his front. My front to the wall.

His fingers against my shoulders push me to the wall and then lightly drag against my skin underneath the band of my bra.

He lifts my hair and whispers a kiss at the base of my neck.

Fingers drag along the straps and his mouth flows wet heat down my spine from neck to band and then glimmers into the deep core of me.

Fingers drag across the top of the band from side to center and two fingers undo the hooks.

Fortunately my hands are above my head, pressed to the wall or my knees might give way.

This journey in its repetition increases the depth of my response, anticipation building excitement.

Excitement building more anticipation.

When the bra goes, I will know that this is not just a flirt before dinner.

The bra off is part of his signal to me that we are moving to another even deeper layer of the ritual.

"Babe," he growls – the timber of his voice reverberating in his chest and across my skin.

In one motion he lifts my bra up and off.

His fingertips press firmly into my back and push me against the wall.

What felt smooth to my back feels deliciously rough to my nipples, hard and teased in the drag across the texture.

His finger drags across the tops of my thighs, creating space between me and the wall.

His fingers slide into the indented space just under each breast.

He brings the same torturing finger drag circle as he presses into me, dragging each nipple again across the roughness.

Skin to skin, his hands support my flesh.

His intentional movement continues the drag of my nipples along the wall.

He lifts my arms above my head and secures the red silk rope, fixed there for just this purpose.

The soft material reminding me of past suspensions, anchoring more anticipation.

His finger drags across my butt.

Then he surprises me as his hand slaps my butt to my right and then another slap to my left.

He rubs himself against me and steps back to slap me once, twice.

Another motion of his skin against me, touching me deeply.

He steps back and delivers another set of slaps.

My skin is buzzing with heat.

"Perfect," he breathes. "Now you match the wall."

The slaps have deepened the effect of his touch.

His fingers begin at my wrists, at the edges of the silk.

Slowly descending, his fingers drag and occasionally circle and press and push inward – sizzling movements meant to keep my awareness on his drag and his connection.

The drag continues down the sides of my body.

As the descent continues, he hooks the elastic waist band of my yoga pants and takes them with.

His knee knocks my knee and I lift each foot to step out as his foot pushes my clothing away.

His fingers return to the sides of my body, tracing circles across my hips and my butt still matching the wall.

He slowly sinks as his tongue trails down my back until it finds the valley between the cheeks of my ass.

Fingers drag up and down on legs and butt.

The wet heat of his tongue fills my need and his for his exercise of free reign with me.

Willingly leaving the shallows for depth, I trust him completely.

That he will push me, excites us both.

That he will surprise me with both the known and the unspoken, ramps the challenge and the response, and deepens our connection.

His fingers drag down my legs and then lightly dance across my feet, visiting each toe then each ankle.

His fingers caress the skin on the outside of my legs to return to my ankles and I feel a deep breath exhale across my backside.

He feels like he is gathering himself for the next part.

Finger drag begins the journey up the inside of each leg.

Instinctively I try to step together but his fingers press against my knees stopping my motion.

I have no choice but to do as directed and his finger push makes me step out a bit more.

Clear awareness of the cool air on my upper, inner thighs moves in just as his thumbs caress this tender skin.

His thumbs reach for the intricate, inner joint between leg and butt and what lies above.

His nose nests into the lower crevice of my butt.

His deep breath inhales my wet and the induced body fragrance of his finger drag.

With my legs pushed apart I am barely balanced on my toes.

Without the wall and his fingers, I would twist and turn.

But I can't. I won't.

I am suspended in the delicious drag, anticipating his next motion.

His nose keeps me pinned.

His thumb lightly traces the edge of my lower lip.

Lips puffy with heat, moist from the unending drag.

The slowness of his digit is excruciating as he moves back to front.

I find myself wanting to pull away at the same time I try to move closer yet stopped by his nose and the red silk.

He has me where he has been maneuvering since his call and his first finger drag.

Lost in the feeling and the motion, literally suspended in time, I jerk in surprise.

A long finger has forcefully penetrated my wet core.

Now finger drag across the internal mound of my pussy.

Intent. Slow. Igniting even more heat.

I am always amazed at his patience, his willingness to go slow yet insistent with every touch and every glide.

A circling, a tugging, a finger which knows, a finger which entreats me to come – to him.

More flame.

More liquid response.

I whimper.

I shiver.

Then just as suddenly that finger drags itself out of me.

I twist turning but suspended.

I lack the momentum to resist his fingers trailing again at my opening.

His thumb continues to trace my pussy lips.

Front to back, back to front, avoiding the button hard from his drag.

His hands push my legs even further apart.

His fingers caress my inner thighs.

I tremble.

My focus fully on his fingers and the motion I hope he is preparing.

His forefinger slowly – slowly – traces my opening and then pushes into the darkness.

Two fingers.

Now three.

Opening. Spreading. Dragging.

I am pushed to my edge.

I am damp and hot.

His fingers follow the flow slowly pulling across my opening, looking for more.

Fingers drill in, mining both my wet and my hot.

"Oh! Babe!" I groan, no longer able to remain quiet.

He rises, dragging hands along my front.

He finds nipples to rub and pull.

I twist and push against the hardness of his body.

Loosing myself, the pull extracts a groan from me.

His tongue tastes the hollow of my neck as he pulls hard on my nipples.

His hand drags the contour of my upper body, down to my hips.

A kiss to my lower spine.

Now hands descend to encircle each ankle, thumbs massaging.

His fingers drag, pushing my legs away, until one finger pushes into my heated wetness.

Again, seeking, pushing, dragging.

But just for a moment because both hands return to my ankles and then drag up my inner legs until only one finger is inserted once again.

Finger dragging, tickling, probing.

His finger at my core pushes me this way and that.

With his finger buried I feel his breath blow across my back.

I twist more, grinding into his finger, pushing against the wall to drag nipples against roughness.

I no longer feel empty of touch.

I no longer need dream because the reality of his finger is always his gift of touch.

Together we share, both getting what we each need from his finger here and his finger there.

Motion and feeling melting together, obliterating external awareness.

Rising, he kisses my shoulder.

His tongue traces the edge of my ear.

I shiver again within his heated breath.

"Babe," he whispers. "I am considering our options."

His hands grasp my ass.

His fingers pulling on my heated skin.

"I know you like me from behind," he whispers.

I twist and he steadies me against the wall.

A hand tugs a nipple.

The pressure building.

My need for release encountering my edge, ready to topple.

"Shall I take you just like this?"

Before I can answer he rolls my nipple with his finger, pulling.

"Or maybe I should put you on all fours, legs spread."

He pulls and tugs.

A finger from my front pushes in to drag my clit.

I'm at the edge, trigger ready.

"You are so wet – I feel you almost ready to go."

Now three fingers enter pumping, pushing, dragging.

I almost let go but instead I breathe deeply and hold myself back.

I know he is testing, teasing, wanting to know the depth of my desire.

"Well, Sugar, what will it be?"

I pause.

I take another breath to draw out the moment, to extend his anticipation, and stoke his heat.

"I want my own treat," I breathe.

Outcome the fingers.

He reaches up and unhooks my wrists.

Pivoting us about 90 degrees, he pushes to bend me at my hips.

He slides me into the sling of our special swing.

A swing with a red silk seat just wide enough to support me but not enough to restrain my breasts, now free to enjoy the swing and the breeze and his easy access.

Positioned to the height of his hips, but too high for my toes to touch the ground.

He reaches across me for the silk restraints hooked by more red silk rope to the wall.

In go both wrists, pulling my arms out and away.

These restraints create tension and resistance and no way for me to escape.

He lifts my legs, steeping between, his fingers grasping my knees.

I am breathless because I know his next move.

With just a slight pull and swing, he buries his shaft into my core.

But he is far from done and will now take advantage of our swing for my treat.

Using my legs for leverage, he swings me away and my pussy clenches, grasping at what is no longer there.

Swing in and his shaft buries itself again.

Holding, pulling we connect, melded together.

His tip dragging across my inner depths.

Every internal surface massaged and touched.

He holds on to my legs and swings me back and forth.

The momentum of the swing drives his cock into me deeper and deeper with each movement.

My restrained wrists at the perfect distance for maximum impact.

Pulled tight, his finger again finds my clit.

Not forgotten, just something he likes to leave for last because he knows me and has learned me.

The anticipation of when draws out my pleasure.

His tease, his rhythm designed just for me, adding dimension to all that has been, a harbinger of what is to come.

The drag pulls me in, pushing at my edge.

He stops the swing as one hand reaches in to finger my hard knob and the other to pull at a nipple.

A hardness which softens our borderline and begins to fuel release.

Another finger finds a nipple to tug and twist.

His cock fills me beyond.

Twist and drag, pulling and pushing.

"That's right, Sugar. Let your sweetness take you."

His fingers increase pressure and speed.

Nipples swell in the yank, creating a line of connection from nipple to clit.

He drags and he pulls.

I can't pinpoint the origination but somewhere along the line he has created and inner vibration builds, connecting sensation across my body, building sweet tension at my core.

A deep pulse which rises within me drawn forward by the tuning of his drag.

Until … from this moment … to this moment: I explode.

Like the run of fingers up the keyboard, the trill of motion running up the keys of my response.

Muscles vibrating, core firing.

Each step a tremor. Each push a treble which hits the border and like a star releases an explosion of light.

Now a dam breaking, I feel the river flood, liquid trailing down my thighs, lusciously fingered to my core.

Lights across our line translate to sound and motion.

I dive into the incredible sensation of his finger dragging across the depth of my soul.

And … he doesn't stop.

He continues the connection, strumming the line, playing me.

His fingers drag along the outside of my legs.

Swing in and out.

Then he withdraws and his fingers push into my quivering core.

His finger drags across my spongy wall.

"Oh! Babe!" I scream.

He slaps my butt and his inner finger drag swings me in.

Another energized slap and I return to the edge, to the building heat, searching another ebb of this tide.

His fingers know me.

He knows when to push, to demand, to not let me avoid the repetition he knows he can expect and he can demand.

Giving over to him, letting him lead is a path of ignition for me.

It's in the guidance to union which brings out the depth within me.

In trust, he controls, and he cajoles, eager to have me come over and over again.

His fingers tip me and once again I explode trailing stars across the sky.

Lifting my legs, he swings me towards him perfectly impaling me on his cock now swelled in size, filling me, rubbing my molten walls.

With each push out, the return swing digs deeper.

Now his cock does the drag.

His stiff shaft fingering and tracing my inner muscles.

This drag is more intense, more direct, more fierce – and completely under his choice.

He does not hesitate to dominate our swing.

Each wave creating, intensifying the line between us.

A line of connection begun in the first drag of his finger.

A line to pull us both together, sharing the same river, building the same heat.

I squeeze my inner muscles, holding him, increasing our friction.

I feel him swell.

Sensing my rhythmic need, he swings my body to the beat of his heart.

Building a coasting drag for us both to ride.

He feels me build.

Every swing a pull of him into me.

Every swing a push of me dragging at him.

His ritual a willingness to take us down, and in, and out.

Where heart meets body and mind meets soul.

Aligned, seen, accepted, embraced.

Finger drag joins us.

Lost in the swing, our inner torrents build.

In the push and pull, the beginnings of release.

A single line between creates the union.

Now cuts us free to follow our deepest response.

I lose awareness of all but his swing, his cock dragging me, his pole pushing me until I lose myself in his touch.

Deep within the torrent builds.

I hear myself groan.

"Harder!"

His cock a huge sword swinging in me, fencing, taunting.

A motion lost in the timelessness.

A motion which frees my mind and then frees my body just for him.

The swing of him in me cuts me free.

I need do nothing more than accept his gift.

Cascades within find release to flow freely.

Together we swing.

Together exploding in the motion, tracing together our mutual release.

He explodes and this explosive drag invites me to join.

A space for me within him.

In the intimate world he has created for us both.

I am free.

I am freed.

I swing as I come.

I bring him into me, receiving all that he gives.

He too comes willingly, pumping, accepting all that I bring.

Like the notes of a song playing in our hearts, bodies unwavering, fingers touching.

Against the red wall, a mutual gift of union – together, in the finger drag of our swing.

ABOUT MARLAYNA

Me, I like my margaritas skinny, my pillows firm, and my men like mountains.

After divorce, I found myself at the crossroads between spiritual being and sexual being — finding that the two are not separate experiences within me.

Sacred Hot is my way of exploring and merging the celestial with the intimate, claiming authentic life on all levels body, mind, heart, and soul.

Learn more on my website: SacredHot.com

Keep up with my new releases and get a free Sacred Hot short story:

https://www.sacredhot.com/newsletter/

Follow me on my Amazon Author page:

https://smile.amazon.com/Marlayna-Fire/e/B084C312NS/

www.ingramcontent.com/pod-product-compliance
Lightning Source LLC
Chambersburg PA
CBHW070105280626

47159CB00016B/1345